THE RIVER SEINE KILLINGS

By Simon McCleave

A DI Ruth Hunter Crime Thriller

Book 10

Your FREE book is waiting for you now!

Get your FREE copy of the prequel to
the DI Ruth Hunter Series NOW
http://www.simonmccleave.com/vip-email-club
and join my VIP Email Club

SIMON MCCLEAVE

For John and Lynn

PROLOGUE
5th November 2013

A strikingly attractive woman in her 30s stood on the platform waiting for her train with the other commuters. Sarah Goddard was pretty, with high cheekbones that accentuated her perfectly arched eyebrows and sparkling chestnut eyes. Bright red lipstick was the only makeup she wore. Her platinum-blonde hair was short, feathered and shaved a little into the nape of her neck. Friends said she looked like a pop star or an actress. She watched a crisp packet dance along in the strong breeze before it dived onto the leaf-strewn tracks. She looked around as the train announcements burbled from tannoys, and people read papers and paperbacks, used their phones, and avoided eye contact or, in fact, any human contact. It's like being in a crowd of robots, *she thought.*

Situated in the London Borough of Bromley, Crystal Palace railway station was opened in 1854 to serve the new site of the 1851 Great Exhibition building, The Crystal Palace, after it was moved from its original location in Hyde Park. Now, every year, it took two and a half million passengers north to Victoria, Wandsworth, West Norwood and Streatham Hill, or south to Beckenham and Norwood.

The wind whipped erratically across Platform 1 as commuters stood almost shoulder to shoulder waiting for the 08.05 to London Victoria.

Sarah usually made herself oblivious to the chaos and uncomfortable nature of commuting to London by listening to loud music or scrolling through social media on her phone. But not today.

Today she just couldn't concentrate. The ball of nerves in her stomach was making her feel sick. She just needed to keep it together.

She was feeling overwhelmed as the train pulled in with a noisy metallic rattle. It was Groundhog Day for every other commuter waiting there. Routine. She knew that most of them even stood at the same place on the platform, got into the same carriage, and stood or sat in their favoured place. Making different choices required effort, and they had a long interminable day ahead of them in the capital where many difficult decisions had to be made. Best to keep this part of the day nice and simple.

The train doors opened with a hiss. Sarah's carriage of choice was already busy and there were no vacant seats. Nothing new there, *she thought. Except today everything felt different. Everything was going to be different and she couldn't do anything about it. She took a sharp intake of breath.*

She stepped on tentatively as she checked her phone. A text from her girlfriend, Ruth.

Meeting Jess and Andy for the fireworks display on Clapham Common outside the Windmill Pub at 7.30pm. See you there. Love you sooooo much xx.

Tears came into her eyes as she read the message several times. She couldn't believe that this was actually happening.

Then she looked up and saw a face. Someone she recognised. A tall man, blonde hair, well-groomed, preppy glasses, wearing an expensive charcoal-coloured suit under a navy Crombie coat with a red lining and its distinctive velvet collar. The sight of him made what was happening all the more real. She could feel herself beginning to shake.

He nodded a confident hello. The train doors closed and then the 08.05 to Victoria pulled out of the station.

'It's Sarah, isn't it?' the man asked. He had a German accent.

'Yes,' she whispered, uncertain of what she was supposed to say to him. Why was he talking to her?

'Don't you remember?' the man answered with a self-assured but unnerving smile.

Of course she remembered him.

The last time she had seen him was the worst day of her life.

CHAPTER 1
Manchester Airport, 2020

Ruth showed her boarding pass to a grinning, heavily made-up member of the French cabin crew who gestured to the sixth row down. The 11.10 Air France flight from Manchester into Charles De Gaulle Airport in Paris would take about an hour. She could feel the knot of nerves in her stomach. It felt surreal that last night she had managed to speak to Sarah for the first time in seven years. Now, just over twelve hours later, she was on a plane heading for Paris in the hope that she could find Sarah and bring her home at last.

At the moment, all Ruth knew was that Sarah had been working for Global Escorts in Paris over recent months. When the premises were raided by the French authorities, the entire operation had already been moved to a 500-acre farm close to the Forêt de Sénart, which was south of Paris. Sarah had managed to reveal in the phone call that she was being kept against her will on that farm. The French authorities believed a man named Patrice Le Bon, who they suspected of international human trafficking, was also the man behind Global Escorts, along with Russian billionaire Sergei Saratov.

Since Sarah's phone call, things had become a little more complicated. The French seemed to have two different police forces. The Police Nationale was responsible for all major French cities and urban areas and was under the control of the Ministry of the Interior. The Paris Police was, however, a separate unit within the Police Nationale and virtually autonomous. Then there was the Gendarmerie Nationale who was part of the French armed forces and was responsible for rural areas such as the Forêt de Sénart. When you added in the interest of the DGSE, Direction Générale De La Sécurité Extérieure, the French equivalent of MI5, who was also keen to bring Le Bon to justice, it made for a bureaucratic nightmare. Ruth was concerned that any attempt to rescue Sarah from the farmhouse might be jeopardised by French authorities' inability to agree who was in charge of the operation. She had seen that sort of thing in the UK before. A criminal operation where both the police and armed forces are deployed, who then have to seek guidance from the Home Office as to who takes the lead.

As Ruth took her seat, she was pleased to see how much legroom there was. The last time she had flown out of the UK was on a budget airline, and even at 5ft 6in her legs had been squashed.

'Hi,' said a male voice with a French accent. It was a middle-aged man in a designer, charcoal-grey suit sitting at the window seat of her row. He was dark, with swept-back greying hair and fashionable glasses.

'Hi,' Ruth replied with a polite smile. She didn't want to appear rude but she also didn't want to get into a conversation for the next hour. Her head was buzzing with everything that had happened over the past twelve hours. She was hoping for some peace and quiet to try and process it all.

The man smiled as he pulled out his laptop.

Oh that's good. Looks like he's going to work during the flight. Then he turned to her again. 'First time to Paris?'

Ruth shook her head. 'No, but I haven't been for a long time.'

1995 to be precise. She and her ex-husband Dan had got the ferry over with friends and driven down to Paris for a club night. They had gone to Le Queen nightclub which was on Avenue des Champs-Élysées. They had seen 'Dimitri From Paris', one of Dan's favourite DJs.

'Business or pleasure?' the man asked, with a slightly creepy grin.

Bloody hell. If only you knew!

Ruth gave a big, unsubtle yawn. 'I'm not sure yet.'

The man opened his laptop. 'Looks like you need some sleep?'

'Yes, I really do,' Ruth replied as she sat back and closed her eyes.

What an incredible story I could tell him. It would blow his mind, she thought. *I'm going to Paris to rescue my ex-partner, the love of my life, Sarah, who went missing seven years ago.* The date of that event was etched on Ruth's mind like the chiselled date on a tombstone. *5th November 2013.* It was the day that Sarah boarded the 08.05 commuter train from Crystal Palace station to London Victoria but never arrived. She had disappeared. No contact, no note, no idea where she had gone. As a copper, Ruth had made sure the CCTV footage from that day had been scoured. Every station on that line had been searched. There had been television appeals and articles in the press. There had been sightings of Sarah from all around the world. Ruth had even followed women she thought looked like Sarah, but she had simply vanished off the face of the earth.

For the first five years, Ruth had heard nothing. However, since then she had uncovered the identity of the man that Sarah was seen talking to on that train to Victoria. Jurgen Kessler. Not only a rich, successful German banker, but a man wanted in connection with two unsolved murders in Berlin. Kessler's trail had led her to discover that Sarah had had an affair with Jamie Parsons, a wealthy businessman and proprietor of the *Secret Garden* sex parties for the rich and powerful. That in turn led to connections with a Russian billionaire, Sergei Saratov, who was suspected of trafficking women into an exclusive ski resort where he owned several hotels.

Ruth's first major breakthrough had occurred when she found CCTV which showed Sarah entering The Dorchester Hotel in London in 2015 with Sergei Saratov. It proved, for the first time, that Sarah hadn't been attacked or murdered on the train from Crystal Palace in November 2013. However, it posed a whole new set of questions. Saratov had been implicated in various trafficking crimes, as well as allegations of sexual assault. Ruth had no idea what Sarah's relationship to Saratov was. With the help of Met Missing Persons Officer Stephen Flaherty, Ruth eventually tracked Sarah down to an elite escort agency, Global Escorts, in Paris. And that was where Ruth had her first glimpse of Sarah in over seven years during a FaceTime call. Before Sarah had chance to respond, the screen had gone blank, Ruth heard Sarah scream, and the call ended. Despite endless tracking by Ruth and then the Met Police Missing Persons Unit, the number couldn't be traced and the Global Escorts website had been closed down.

Then last night, Sarah had called her from the farmhouse where she was being held. They had only spoken for seconds, but Ruth promised Sarah she was coming to Paris to find her and take her home.

And so, here she was.

The flight into Paris had been blissfully uneventful. Gazing out of the window of her taxi, Ruth now watched the Parisienne suburbs go by. She hadn't realised that it was nearly twenty miles from Charles De Gaulle Airport to central Paris. It didn't matter. It gave her time to compose her thoughts before meeting with her contacts from the Paris Police and Interpol.

The A1 motorway into the city was flat and soulless. The road was bordered by identical one-storey warehouses and was busy with lorries ferrying goods for companies she had never heard of. It wasn't until they got to the northern suburb of Saint-Denis that it became clear they were on the outskirts of a city.

'First time in Paris?' the taxi driver asked. He was dark skinned, with a short beard, and had spent the journey so far talking to someone on the hands-free phone in a language she didn't understand. If she were to take a guess, then she would have said it was Arabic, possibly Algerian Arabic. Given France's colonial connections to that country, she knew there were many Algerians in France. In fact, she was pretty sure that French was their official language.

'No, but I haven't been for a long time,' Ruth answered.

'I think you will find it has changed a lot,' he suggested, shaking his head. 'Too many of these immigrants in Paris now. It is no good.'

'Right.' He clearly didn't class himself as an immigrant, which was interesting.

'Portuguese, Spanish, Germans, they're everywhere,' he explained. 'My grandfather came here in 1971. He dug and laid tracks for the Metros. So did my father. But those jobs have gone to these immigrants because they are EU citizens. I have friends who are even going back to Algiers. It is crazy.'

Ruth tried to be diplomatic. 'I'm originally from London. I think all big cities have these problems.'

'London? It is a good city, no?'

Ruth shrugged. 'Not always. It's good and bad, like everywhere I suppose.'

'I like Arsenal. The football team? The Gunners!' he announced with a broad grin. 'You like Arsenal?'

'No.' She shook her head. 'My family all support Chelsea. South London.'

'Chelsea.' He gave a little laugh. 'Yes, they are a good team also.'

The taxi driver waited outside her hotel in Montmartre while she checked in and quickly unpacked her case in her room.

The next fifteen minutes of the journey were spent in a comfortable silence as the taxi weaved its way towards La Préfecture, a huge building in the Place Louis Lépine on the Île de la Cité in the centre of the city. Although La Préfecture de Police de Paris was a unit of the French Ministry of the Interior, it was essentially the building that symbolised the police force of Paris, and was therefore the equivalent of Scotland Yard.

Once she had added the tip, Ruth got no change from the €50 note she had handed to her amiable taxi driver, who gave her a toothy grin and a wave as he sped away into the noisy Parisienne traffic.

Fifty bloody Euros! she thought. *That's virtually fifty quid isn't it?*

Gazing up at the enormous neo-Florentine 19th century building, she took a breath and composed herself.

Here we go.

CHAPTER 2

The austere fifth floor meeting room was dark and musty, with wooden panelled walls. There were several oil paintings of past Mayors of Paris, as well as a huge bookshelf full of leather-bound books.

It doesn't exactly say 21st century policing, Ruth thought to herself.

She sat at a large but empty oak table where she had been placed by a young woman who seemed confused by her arrival. From the window, Ruth guessed that she was looking north across the city that was now covered by a grey canopy of thick cloud and drizzle. The River Seine flowed left under Pont Neuf. Beyond that, in the distance, she could make out the top of the high-tech 70s architecture of the Pompidou Centre. Behind that, the white Basilique du Sacré-Cœur cut into the skyline.

The heavy wooden door creaked open and a tall man in his 40s entered the room. His raincoat was flecked with rain.

'Detective Inspector Hunter, is that right?' the man asked as he approached her. He was English and well educated. More of a London public day school accent than the true aristocrats of Eton, Harrow or Rugby.

'Yes,' Ruth replied as he shook her hand too firmly.

'Oliver Trelford,' he panted, sounding a little flustered as he sat down. 'Ian has had to go down to Lyon and sends his apologies. I've had a few hours though to look through the files, so I'm relatively up to speed.'

Up to this point, Ian Harrison had been her main point of contact at the Paris branch of Interpol, the International Criminal Police Organisation - or in France, *L'Organisation Internationale de Police Criminelle.* With 194 member states, it was the world's largest international police organisation which facilitated co-operation among law enforcement agencies across the world. Much of their work revolved around maintaining accurate and up-to-date criminal databases and communications networks. Ruth was aware that it wasn't itself a law enforcement agency and therefore had no powers of arrest or detention.

'Oh, right.' Ruth tried to hide her disappointment. Harrison had come across as a smart, no-nonsense man who was very well-briefed about the Paris Police Préfecture's ongoing operation against Patrice Le Bon and Sergei Saratov.

'So, either way, I'm afraid you're lumbered with me,' Trelford informed her with the kind of snort only the English upper middle classes could make.

Oh great. He's not exactly filling me with confidence!

'What do you know about this place in the Forêt de Sénart?' she asked him.

Trelford pulled a face. 'To be honest, I'm guessing you'll know more than me at the moment.'

Oh great. Very reassuring.

The door opened again and a hefty-looking man in his late 50s with black swept-back hair, Gallic nose, and wiry eyebrows approached them. He had an air of annoyance as he sat, placed a laptop and files on the table, and then looked over at Ruth.

'Detective Inspector Hunter?' he enquired as she got a waft of the stale cigarette smoke that heralded his arrival.

She nodded as she put out her hand to shake his. He looked confused, took her hand for less than a second, as though he were picking up a dropped piece of food, and returned his attention to the files in front of him.

I thought the French were meant to be charming?

'And you're from London?' he asked as he shuffled through his files.

'Originally ... I now work in North Wales.'

'Pays de Galles,' he mumbled almost to himself as though this was of no interest to him.

Is that French for Wales? Ruth wondered.

'We've met before,' Trelford informed Vernier, but didn't risk a handshake. 'Capitaine Vernier?'

Vernier raised one of his enormous eyebrows to signify that he had no recollection of Trelford. Then he gave an indifferent nod to confirm his name and fixed Ruth with a stare.

He opened one of the files, took out a coloured map, and turned it so that she and Trelford could see it. He then jabbed a location with one of his thick hairy fingers. 'This farm, to the north of the Forêt de Sénart, is maybe forty kilometres south of here. You think your friend is at this farm, yes?'

She nodded. 'We had a brief conversation on a mobile phone, but yes, I believe she is with other women being held against their will at that location. I understand that you have officers there, is that correct?' Ruth asked, now aware that she had butterflies in her stomach. She just wanted to know what their plans were and when, or if, there was going to be a rescue attempt.

'Yes, of course,' Vernier stated in a tone that suggested he thought it was a stupid question. 'We have had this farm under surveillance for three days now.'

'And you're convinced that this is where the women are being held?' Trelford asked.

Vernier nodded as he opened the laptop, turned it on, and brought up video footage on the screen. Even though the recording was a little blurred, it clearly showed a group of five women sitting at a table on a large terrace to the rear of a farmhouse. Several of them were smoking. In the background, two men stood talking and one of them was visibly armed with some kind of assault rifle slung over his shoulder. 'Do you recognise any of these women please?'

Peering at the screen, Ruth searched their faces. Their ages seemed to range from late teens to about thirty – but Sarah wasn't one of them. Her stomach lurched. What if Sarah had been mistaken? What if she wasn't there? What if they had taken her somewhere else?

She shook her head. 'No, sorry.'

Vernier clicked another MPEG file and another shaky piece of footage played. 'What about this?'

Two women, wearing sunglasses, were sitting on a bench deep in conversation.

Staring at the woman on the left of the screen, Ruth realised that she recognised her.

Oh my God!

It was Sarah.

'Yes, that's Sarah Goddard,' she whispered as a surge of anxiety and excitement shot through her body.

Vernier nodded as though this just confirmed what he already knew. 'I understand that you haven't seen her for a long time?'

'Nearly seven years.'

Vernier paused a moment. 'Then maybe you get to see her today.'

Ruth frowned. 'Really?'

Looking at his watch, Vernier got up from the table. 'The rescue operation at the farm is in three hours. If you follow me, we have a meeting. And I will organise transport for you two to travel to the Forêt de Sénart as official observers.'

Ruth's heartbeat quickened as she looked over at Trelford. She wasn't expecting things to be moving that fast.

The Paris Police Nationale briefing room was far more modern than the meeting room they had been in twenty minutes earlier. It also bore many common elements of the incident rooms that Ruth had experienced in her time in the Met and in North Wales. There were scene boards with dates, times and photos, and a large map of the target area with blue pins to indicate key locations. Of course, everything was in French, and her grasp of the language was pretty basic.

Vernier launched into a briefing with another man who was dressed in uniform. Then he paused and looked over at her.

'We also have two observers with us today,' he explained. 'Detective Inspector Hunter from the UK and ...?'

'Oliver Trelford,' Trelford prompted.

'Monsieur Trelford from Interpol,' Vernier announced. 'Detective Inspector Hunter works in Wales.'

Several of the officers in the room turned to look at her, most with friendly smiles and nods. There were some mutterings, and she distinctly heard the phrase *Pays De Galles*, before there was laughter.

Feeling that she might be the butt of some joke, Ruth gave Trelford a dubious look. 'My French is awful. What's so funny?'

Trelford smiled. 'Just a joke about the rugby. It seems that France beat Wales in Cardiff quite recently.'

'Right. No idea,' Ruth said. 'How's your French?'

'I'm bilingual,' Trelford explained, 'I can be your translator for the day.'

She gave him a kind smile. 'Thank you.' She might have misjudged him as he didn't seem quite the public school twit that she had him down as.

As the briefing continued in French, she glanced around the room. A yellow poster on the wall beside her carried a photo of an Arabic-looking man, Omar Animour. Across the top of the poster was *Euro Most Wanted*. There was a list of personal details in French. *Infraction,* which she assumed was French for offence, was listed as *Terrorisme*, which was self-explantory. *Coleur des Yeux* was listed as *Marron*, which she didn't know, but by looking at the man's photograph she could see that he had dark brown eyes.

Isn't that brun in French? she thought.

Ruth's attention was broken as an officer entered the room and came over to speak to Vernier in hushed tones.

She turned to Trelford. 'Do you know what's going on?'

He shook his head as Vernier looked out at the assembled room and began to speak in a serious voice.

After he had finished, Trelford turned to her. 'Did you catch any of that?'

Ruth shook her head blankly. 'Not a word.'

'Intelligence officers have just reported that there seems to be movement from inside the farmhouse,' he revealed. 'From what they can see, it appears that everyone inside is packing up. They look like they're getting prepared to leave.'

'They're on the move?'

'That's what they think,' he confirmed.

Ruth took a deep breath. The news had only served to heighten her anxiety.

Trelford gave her a wry smile. 'Sounds like they were tipped off.'

'You don't seem surprised?'

'I'm not,' he said with an ironic laugh. 'I've been in France for ten years. Someone is always tipping someone else off. It's part of the culture. Le monde ne sera pas détruit par ceux qui font le mal, mais par ceux qui les regardent sans rien faire.'

'What does that mean?' Ruth asked.

'The world will not be destroyed by those who do evil, but by those who watch them without doing anything.'

CHAPTER 3

Nearly an hour later, Ruth and Trelford were hammering down the N6 motorway south out of Paris. Sitting in the back of the dark blue Renault Megane, Ruth took out a cigarette. Her nerves were jangling and her need to smoke was getting the better of her.

Trelford had spent most of the journey engrossed in the case files or sending messages and emails on his phone. A French police officer, who stared silently at the road ahead, was at the wheel and talked into his radio at regular intervals.

'Anyone mind if I smoke if I wind down the window?' she asked sheepishly.

'No, of course not,' Trelford replied without looking up. He then mumbled something in French to the driver who shrugged to indicate he didn't mind.

She lowered the window, cupped her hand, lit the cigarette and took a deep drag.

That's a bit better.

Trelford smiled. 'You look like you needed that.'

'Yeah, I really did,' she conceded with a self-effacing laugh.

'I take it you worked in the Met before you went up to North Wales?'

She wasn't sure that she was in the mood for a *getting to know you* type of conversation, but the tension of the journey was starting to feel a little overwhelming.

'Twenty-five years,' she stated with an element of pride.

'Blimey, that must have been tough?' he asked with genuine interest.

She nodded as some of the more harrowing experiences flashed across her mind's eye. 'Yeah, it was a little bit hairy at times.'

'Hairy? Good word,' he laughed. 'I read a paper the other week that had Peckham down as the most dangerous borough in London.'

Blowing a plume of smoke out of the car's window, she watched as it whipped away in the passing air stream.

'I'm guessing North Wales is very different?' Trelford asked after a few seconds.

He's clearly not someone who likes to sit in silence, she thought.

'It is *very* different in lots of ways. But it's not how I thought it was going to be,' she admitted, immediately wondering why she had chosen to reveal such a personal thought.

'Why not?'

She shrugged as she flicked the remainder of the cigarette out of the window and buzzed it up. 'I naively assumed that crime would be at a much lower level. And I also arrogantly anticipated less sophistication in both the criminals and my fellow police officers. Turns out I was completely wrong.'

'Does that mean you regret moving away from the Met?' he asked.

The question stumped her for a few seconds. She couldn't remember anyone ever asking her that in such a direct way. What did she really think?

'No, I don't regret it one bit,' she admitted instinctively. 'I work with some fantastic officers. I live in a very quiet little Welsh village where everyone says hello or stops to chat. There are still major crimes, but I'm glad I made the move.'

Trelford gestured to the case files. 'I hope you don't mind me saying, but I'm guessing that moving to North Wales was a way of dealing with what had happened to your friend Sarah too?'

'She wasn't my friend,' Ruth stated. 'She was my partner. We lived together.'

'Yes, I know. It just wasn't for me to describe her as your partner.'

Emotionally intuitive too? He's full of surprises, isn't he?

'You guessed right,' she conceded quietly. 'I hoped that moving to Wales would help, but all that baggage comes with you, however hard you try to leave it behind.'

'I guess it does.' Trelford looked directly at her. 'So, all this is incredibly important for you today? You must be feeling very emotional?'

Before she had time to answer, they took a sharp turn and drove down a dusty, bumpy track that took them into a wooded area.

Their police driver stopped the car, turned, mumbled something to Trelford and gestured for them to get out.

Glancing outside, Ruth could see a line of police cars.

A black Mercedes van reversed and a group of men jumped out. They were dressed all in black, with helmets, balaclavas, perspex visors, body armour and Heckler & Koch G36 assault rifles. They looked almost identical to the Authorised Firearms Officers from the UK police. Ruth knew they were officers from RAID, which stood for *Recherche, Assistance, Intervention, Dissuasion* - the elite tactical firearms unit of the French National Police.

'Looks like we're here.' Ruth then opened the car door with some trepidation.

Vernier, who was now wearing a Kevlar bulletproof vest, approached as they got out. He was holding two more vests.

'You want to come with us, or you want to stay here?' he grumbled.

Trelford held up his hands as his eyes widened. 'Hey, I'm more than happy to stay here out of the line of fire.'

Ruth looked at Vernier. 'I'm coming with you,' she announced emphatically.

Trelford pulled a face. 'Really? Is that wise?'

She raised an eyebrow. 'I've been waiting for this moment for seven years.'

Vernier gave her his usual crabby expression and tossed the vest over to her. 'Here. You wear this but I cannot give you a firearm.'

Slipping on the heavy vest, Ruth nodded. 'That's fine.'

Vernier gestured to her impatiently. 'Come on. We are going now.'

Trelford looked at her. 'Good luck.'

'Thanks,' Ruth faltered as her heart thudded against her chest.

Let's do this. Let's go and get her.

Sitting in the back of one of the armed response vehicles, Ruth looked out at the forest as they drove slowly along the dusty track and up towards the farmhouse. Inside the vehicle were four heavily-armed RAID officers in full combat gear.

The Mercedes hit a pothole and she grabbed the leather strap that hung from the van's roof to stop her from falling forward. The bulletproof vest felt heavy and restrictive, and it dug painfully into her armpits. She thought of all the uncomfortable hours she had cursed *bloody bulletproof vests*, but she also remembered how a very similar vest had saved her life during a police operation at Solace Farm in Snowdonia not that long ago.

A crackle and a voice on the radio broke the tense silence inside the van.

The vehicle smelled of stale cigarettes, coffee, and gun oil.

Ruth could feel the adrenaline surging through her body. It was making her feel agitated.

She glanced quickly at the RAID officer next to her, and got a waft of his deodorant or shower gel. He stared at the floor, readying himself for the operation.

She looked back to the uneven track behind. Even at their restricted speed, they were leaving a cloud of dust in their wake.

Two more RAID vehicles were following, each with more armed officers.

Their driver spoke into the radio as they turned a corner and saw the large farmhouse ahead of them. The enormous wrought iron gates were wide open but the yard in front of the house was deserted.

As they drove slowly through the gates, she heard the sound of the RAID officers clicking off the safety catches on their assault rifles.

There was a growing knot in her stomach as the van pulled to a halt in the yard and the two doors slid open very slowly.

Ruth unclipped her seatbelt.

The officer next to her gestured silently to the open door with his gloved hand.

Getting out slowly, she felt the dry earth crunch underneath her shoes. The air was hot and dusty, with the scent of olive trees. With dark irony, she thought it smelled like being on holiday somewhere in the Mediterranean.

Bloody hell! If only!

She gazed up at the traditional French farmhouse. A few of the shuttered windows on the first floor were slightly ajar but there seemed to be no one around.

Where is everyone?

The trees to the right shook gently in the wind and then stopped as if they had registered their presence.

She heard the faint sound of a goat in the distance.

Then another gentle whoosh as the wind picked up again, and fallen leaves swirled and danced around the yard.

The silence was starting to spook her.

Glancing to her left, she watched eight RAID officers fan out as they moved forward cautiously in a crouching position.

Maybe the occupants of the farmhouse had seen them coming and were hiding, ready to defend themselves?

There was a glint of sunlight from a pane of glass as one of the windows opened fully.

Shit! Someone is watching us from inside.

Ruth felt her pulse quicken as she watched Vernier and three officers approach the front door.

It's way too quiet, she thought. *They know we're here.*

Vernier took the handgun from the holster on his belt and knocked loudly on the wooden door.

Nothing.

Somewhere behind one of those windows or doors was Sarah.

Come on. Come on, Ruth thought impatiently.

Moving out from behind the van, she crept towards the farmhouse and peered through a downstairs window.

Sarah was in there.

The sight of the armed officers and their weapons was making her feel sick. She didn't want Sarah getting caught in some deadly crossfire.

Scanning the breadth of the farmhouse, Ruth couldn't see a single movement anywhere to indicate anyone was inside.

Then she had a horrible thought. Had they managed to leave the farmhouse under the cover of night and disappeared?

Vernier knocked again and waited.

Inhaling deeply to calm her nerves, Ruth looked over at the RAID officers who had spaced themselves across several downstairs windows. She saw them take out their stun grenades and prepare them.

One of the officers shook his head at Vernier to indicate he hadn't seen any movement.

Vernier clicked his radio and spoke quietly in French as he took a few steps away from the farmhouse and looked up at the first floor again.

BANG! CRACK! CRACK! BANG!

The air above Ruth seemed to explode like a deafening fireworks display.

Shouting, glass breaking, a scream.

What the hell is going on?

As she turned to run for cover behind the Mercedes van, something punched her hard between the shoulder blades and tossed her to the ground.

Spitting dirt from her mouth, she tried to suck in breath. *I've been shot!*

The bullet had hit the back of her vest and winded her. *Get up! Get up!*

As she rolled over, she was still gasping. *Jesus, I'm suffocating!*

At last she gulped a lungful of air. *Thank God!*

The sound of gunfire was earsplitting.

She rolled onto her side and tried to get up but she was dizzy.

Vernier appeared, grabbed the top of her vest, and pulled her away from the farmhouse.

The air was full of deafening noise and the smell of cordite.

Scrambling to her feet, she turned to thank him as he shouted commands into his radio.

Suddenly the air was filled with noise and flames. The windows along the front of the farmhouse exploded in an eruption of fire and glass.

Ruth was lifted by the force of the explosion and landed heavily on her back. *Jesus! What the hell just happened?*

For a moment, everything seemed to be silent. An eerie darkness, as if all the light had been drained from the sky.

Ruth couldn't hear anything but a low hum.

The air was hot and thick.

Drawing in breath, all she could smell was dust and explosives.

And then a strange sense of rain as bits of stone from the farmhouse fell silently all around.

Ruth choked for a moment and looked up at Vernier. His face was slightly blackened. He said something but there was still ringing in her ears.

She looked at the farmhouse in a daze - it was now engulfed in a blazing, flaring cauldron of fire.

Then everything went black.

CHAPTER 4

Blinking open her eyes, Ruth tried to focus on what was directly above her. At first, she thought she was somehow submerged under water. She was struggling to breathe, and the sounds of people talking around her were no more than distorted noises, like warped notes from a musical score. A mumbling audio tapestry which seemed to reverberate deep inside her eardrum and head, like the noise you got when you tried to speak under water.

Where the hell am I? she thought, trying to fight her way back to consciousness. Her temples were throbbing as though she had some dreadful hangover.

A large circular light appeared above her, making her squint. Her vision was still cloudy and fogged but the sensation of being under water had now gone. She was cold, and felt a gust of wind blow across her face. It smelled fresh and clean. To her right, she could just make out the light clink and clank of small metal objects.

Flexing the fingers on her right hand, she concluded that she was lying on some kind of stretcher or bed. There were cold aluminium rails at each side to prevent her from falling off.

Blinking again, she saw a face peering down at her. A man in a blue surgical mask, cap and gloves. For a few seconds, she was startled by his appearance. He was holding up a scalpel which glinted in the light.

Am I in an operating theatre? What the hell happened to me?

'Ruth?' a voice enquired with a thick French accent.

Am I in a French hospital?

As she tried to move from where she was lying, she realised that every part of her body hurt and ached.

Christ, I feel like I've been run over by a train!

Then it started to come back to her. She remembered being shot in the back and then an explosion – but nothing after that. What had happened? And then a surge of panic. What about Sarah? What happened to Sarah?

Lifting up her head, she saw another man coming towards her dressed in a surgical mask and hat.

'Ruth? Ruth? Are you okay?' His voice was English and familiar.

She squinted at his face.

It was DCI Drake looking at her from behind the mask.

What the hell is he doing here? Oh my God, am I going mad?

However, the voice she could hear wasn't Drake's. It was clipped and well educated. It was Oliver Trelford.

Why is Drake talking with Trelford's voice?

'Ruth?' the voice asked again in a concerned tone.

Closing her eyes tightly, she tried to come out of the semi-consciousness which seemed to lay over her like a thick, heavy blanket.

Very slowly, her vision began to refocus.

The hazy light above had been replaced by the criss-cross of branches and trees. Beyond that, a warm vanilla sunlight and azure sky. The height of the oaks and pines above her seemed overwhelming as she tried to move.

A face appeared above her. It was Trelford. 'Are you okay?' He signalled to a paramedic that she needed attention.

'I'm not sure yet,' she groaned, as the paramedic began to check her over.

As she glanced around, she realised that she was back in the clearing in the Forêt de Sénart where she had left Trelford before travelling up to the farmhouse. She had no memory of how she had got back there. There were ambulances parked up, blue lights flashing silently, and a small army of paramedics tending to several wounded RAID officers and others that she didn't recognise.

Nearby, a group of women were being ushered gently into a police van while handcuffed men were being pushed into the back of police cars.

The air split with a siren as one of the white *Service d'Aide Médicale Urgente,* or SAMU, ambulances sped away towards the motorway.

As she gritted her teeth and sat up on the stretcher, her head felt like it was going to explode. 'What the hell happened?'

'They rigged the place with explosives,' Trelford said grimly. 'By a miracle, only one confirmed fatality. A member of the gang.'

'What about Sarah?' she asked frantically.

Trelford swallowed hard and glanced away for a fleeting moment. The look on his face filled Ruth with a pulsing dread.

'What?' she asked almost hysterically, her eyes looking around wildly at the wounded. 'Was she in the farmhouse?'

'Yes,' he stated quietly, 'they found her locked in a room with five other women.'

'And they got them all out safely?' Ruth asked, her voice holding a note of panic. The anxiety of not knowing what had happened to Sarah was making her feel sick to her stomach.

Trelford hesitated. There was something he wasn't telling her. 'Yes.'

Swinging her legs over the side of the stretcher, Ruth glared at him and gestured to the wounded and to the cars and vans. 'Where is she then?'

The paramedic, who had examined her a minute ago, came over shaking her head and wagging her finger. 'Non, non. Vous devez reposer un peu!'

'She wants you to lie down and rest,' Trelford explained.

Fuck that. I'm finding out what happened to Sarah.

Ruth wasn't in the mood to be told what to do. She needed to see Sarah right now. What the hell was Trelford hiding from her? He said there had only been one fatality.

She stood up, trying to get her balance as the paramedic continued to gesture for her to get back on the stretcher.

'Where the hell is she, Oliver?' she demanded. Her head swayed and pounded as she tried to steady herself.

Trelford looked over to where two paramedics were kneeling on the ground beside the open back door of an ambulance. They were attaching a drip to someone on a stretcher. Whoever it was on there, it didn't look like they were in good shape.

'Jesus!' she stuttered as her voice broke.

Taking two steps forward, she lost her balance and sank to her knees.

'Here you go,' said a voice. It was Vernier.

He put his arm under hers and lifted her. 'Come on. I will take you to her.'

'Is she okay?' Ruth gasped.

'I don't know,' Vernier muttered as he helped her to her feet.

With Vernier taking some of her weight, she hobbled to-wards the paramedics.

A woman was lying on the stretcher under a blanket with orange straps fastened across her body and a brace around her neck.

Her face was covered in blood but Ruth could see it was Sarah.

Oh my God!

It was the first time she had physically laid eyes on her in seven long years.

'Jesus,' she whispered under her breath. 'Is she going to be all right?'

Please God, let her be all right!

Vernier asked the paramedics something in French and they replied.

He looked at her with a solemn expression. 'Your friend has a serious head injury. The doctors at the hospital will tell us more.'

The paramedics lifted the stretcher and put Sarah into the back the ambulance.

As tears filled her eyes, Ruth could feel herself shaking all over as she watched helplessly. 'Where are they taking her?'

'Paris,' Vernier explained. 'Hôpital Européen Georges-Pompidou. It has the best trauma centre in Paris.'

CHAPTER 5

It was early evening, and having been checked over by the paramedics, Ruth had insisted that she be taken straight to the Hôpital Européen Georges-Pompidou, an ultra-modern hospital that lay to the south of the Seine in what was known as the Quartier de Javel.

She was desperate for news of Sarah's condition. Every time the door opened or a doctor walked past, her pulse would quicken. *What's taking them so long?*

The wait was agonising.

What if she dies from her injuries? Surely God wouldn't be cruel enough to let me get this close, after all this time, only to snatch her away like that?

Maybe it was their fate not to be together again. Did she believe in fate? She didn't know what she thought or felt at that moment. She was utterly exhausted, in a great deal of pain, and an emotional, nervous wreck.

Apart from that, I'm fine, she thought to herself sarcastically.

Gazing out of a window in a small side room on the ninth floor of the hospital, Ruth saw the looming presence of the Eiffel Tower that was about two miles to the north. She had only ever managed to get halfway up the tower when she'd visited Paris with Dan in the early 90s. He suffered from terrible vertigo, and headed back to the lift after only five minutes on the viewing platform.

To her left, she could see the huge expanse of the hospital itself. With the exception of the external steel staircases, everything was constructed from glass. It looked more like a modern art gallery or a state-of-the-art five star hotel than a hospital.

Moving across the room, she slumped down onto a long, black sofa. As her back touched its surface, there was a searing pain between her shoulder blades from where she had been shot. It took her breath away.

Jesus! That hurts!

She sat forward, took a long deep breath and looked expectantly at the door.

Come on, come on. Just tell me something.

The door opened slowly and Trelford appeared holding two coffees.

'Thought you could do with one of these,' he suggested as he approached and handed her the cardboard cup.

'Only if it's got whiskey in it,' she quipped dryly.

Trelford looked at her seriously. 'Shouldn't you be resting in your hotel?'

Ruth took a sip of the strong, bitter coffee. It was exactly what she needed. 'No,' she retorted, shaking her head. 'I'm not going anywhere until I see Sarah. Even if I have to sleep on this sofa.'

'I don't think that's a very good idea. He paused for a second, then asked, 'Do you want me to get you anything to eat?'

'No, thanks,' she murmured, now lost in her own thoughts. 'Did the police get the evidence they needed from the farmhouse?'

'No, I'm afraid not. Paperwork, computers, everything went up in the explosion and subsequent fire.'

'How did they know we were coming?'

'What do you mean?'

'That farmhouse had been under surveillance by the Paris Police for three days,' Ruth stated, thinking out loud. 'How did they know the precise timing of the rescue operation?'

Trelford shrugged. 'Maybe they just saw you guys coming up the track?'

She shook her head. 'No way. I've been a police officer for nearly thirty years. That farmhouse was on lockdown and prepared hours before we drove up there. How could they have known that?'

'Sounds like you think they were tipped off?'

'Don't you?' She raised an eyebrow. 'I know there was a previous operation at Global Escorts in central Paris, but by the time the police arrived, the place had been stripped and everyone had vanished.'

'That was definitely a tip-off.' Trelford took a long sip of his coffee. 'They have another saying here.'

'Oh good,' Ruth groaned. 'That's just what I need. Go on.'

'There are so many leaks in Paris that when it rains, it no longer gets wet. It sounds better in French.'

'Can't you do something?' she asked, shaking her head.

'Interpol has no jurisdiction here, no powers of arrest or investigation. We've handed our concerns on to the IGPN ...'

Ruth squinted in confusion – she had no idea what that was.

'Sorry, L'Inspection Générale de la Police Nationale. Effectively their version of internal affairs.'

'And?'

'Nothing. We were whistling in the wind,' he grumbled. 'The IGPN isn't independent and no one trusts it to do its job.

You've basically got French cops investigating French cops, and concluding every time that no one has overstepped the mark.'

Before their conversation could continue, the door opened and a female doctor entered, holding files. She was tall and wore thin-rimmed glasses.

Ruth immediately stood up and approached her. 'I'm waiting for news of my friend, Sophie?'

Ruth had insisted that, for her own safety, Sarah be given an alias while she was at the hospital. She had been registered as Sophie Collins.

The doctor gave her a kind smile. 'Yes. You are the English police officer?'

Ruth nodded but all she really wanted to know was how Sarah was.

'Sophie has suffered a blow to the front of her head but the CAT scan and X-ray show there is no serious damage. Your friend is very lucky. She just has a few bruises and concussion.'

In her highly anxious state, Ruth was trying to process exactly what the doctor had said. 'Does that mean she's going to be okay?'

'Yes,' the doctor reassured her. 'She needs to rest, but she is not in any danger.'

Feeling the tears in her eyes, Ruth took a breath and then whispered, 'Thank you. Thank you so much.'

The doctor gave her a quizzical look. 'Seems like you should go to your hotel and get some rest.'

Ruth wasn't listening. 'Can I see her?'

The doctor shook her head. 'No, I don't think that's a good idea.'

'Please,' Ruth implored her. 'We haven't seen each other for many years ... Please.'

The doctor hesitated, then reached over and touched Ruth's arm. 'I will talk to the nursing staff. You can see Sophie for a few minutes, but no more.'

Ruth and Trelford made their way down to the Unité de Soins Intensifs, the hospital's Intensive Care Unit, on the sixth floor. The unit was quiet and still, with only the electronic bleeps of the equipment as a rhythmical background noise.

'Sophie Collins?' Trelford asked. 'I don't understand.'

'I asked Vernier for her to be registered here under an alias,' Ruth told him. 'I thought it would be safer.'

'Makes sense.' He gestured to some chairs. 'I can wait for you here, if you like?'

'It's okay, Oliver,' she assured him gently. 'Why don't you go home. It's been quite a day.'

He nodded. 'As long as you don't mind?'

'No, of course not. I'll be fine. And thank you for everything today.'

He ran his hands through his hair. 'You're welcome. I'm sure we'll catch up tomorrow. And I'm glad you're getting to see Sarah.'

She watched him go for a few seconds before walking into the reception area of the USI and attracting the attention of a kind-looking nurse who came over and whispered something to her in French.

'Sorry,' Ruth whispered back apologetically. 'My French isn't very good. I am looking for Sophie Collins. She's English.'

The nurse nodded immediately and gestured benignly for her to follow. 'Oui, bien sûr.'

They made their way across the USI towards a small corner room. The nurse opened the door quietly and with her head gestured to the patient in the bed.

Ruth went in, hardly daring to look.

It was Sarah.

Her eyes were closed but her face and hair had been washed clean of the blood. She was attached to several drips and monitors.

But it was her.

The nurse smiled, closed the door and left.

Oh my God! This just doesn't feel real.

Ruth moved slowly across the room, took a chair, and put it down beside the bed. She watched Sarah's chest rise and fall gently, as she had done so many times in the past. Then she looked at the tiny, fawn-coloured mole at the base of her neck, on the right hand side, that she had kissed innumerable times.

I have prayed so hard for this moment to come. And now it has. But I don't know how to feel because it's too much for me to believe it's real.

Ruth sat down and just stared at Sarah's face intently. Her perfect rosebud lips. The soft elfin-like features that Ruth thought she had etched into her memory. She looked the same ... but she also looked different.

You have no idea what I promised to whatever eternal presence looks after us for this moment to happen. For you to be alive.

Moving her unsteady hand forward, she reached out and placed it gently over Sarah's.

It was warm and soft.

In that moment, Ruth felt an overwhelming rush of emotion, like nothing she had ever felt before.

Relief, happiness, love and regret.

Please tell me that I'm not dreaming this time.

She squeezed Sarah's small hand in hers for a second. Then she noticed she was still wearing the black and silver thumb ring she had bought for her. She took a long calming breath. Seeing that ring meant so much. It meant that she hadn't forgotten about Ruth. She hadn't thrown it away in an attempt to forget and eradicate her past.

Glastonbury 2007. That was when Ruth had bought Sarah the ring, from a stall close to the Pyramid Stage. The festival had been a washout but Ruth and Sarah weren't deterred. They had their Hunter wellies and lots of cider – so they just didn't care. Having watched Pete Doherty over on the main stage, they had made their way through the trench-like mud towards the Pyramid Stage, where they were going to watch The Killers play the headline set on Saturday night. They had been killing time, looking through the stalls at bags, hats and multi-coloured raincoats when Ruth spotted the ring. It was £12 and it fitted the thumb on Sarah's right hand perfectly. It was meant to be, an omen, she told Sarah, who wore the ring every day after that.

Ruth felt Sarah's hand move slightly.

Did she just squeeze my hand?

'Hello,' whispered a croaky voice.

Looking up, she saw Sarah squinting and looking down the bed at her.

'Hello, you,' Ruth whispered as her voice broke with emotion.

Oh my God!

Sarah's face broke into a smile as her eyes adjusted to the light.

'Is that really you?' she asked as she squeezed Ruth's hand.

Ruth nodded as her eyes filled with tears. 'Yeah, it's really me.' Blowing out her cheeks, she took a deep breath and dabbed away the tears from her face.

'Where am I?' Sarah mumbled in her gravelly voice.

'A hospital in Paris,' Ruth replied quietly with a sniff. 'There was an explosion at the farmhouse where they were keeping you. Do you remember?'

Sarah smiled at her and shook her head. 'No, but I don't really care. What are you doing here?'

'I told you that I was coming to get you,' Ruth retorted with a laugh.

'Yeah, you did.'

'So, I'm here. Sitting here with you.'

'I know. It's amazing, isn't it?'

They locked eyes for a moment with an overwhelming sense of bewilderment.

'Is this real?' Sarah asked as she shifted awkwardly in the bed.

Ruth shrugged. 'You know what, I have no idea.'

'What's my favourite food?' Sarah asked with a curious smile.

'Sushi. Maybe a Katsu curry,' Ruth stated without hesitation. 'What's mine?'

'You'd like it to be something exotic like Thai Green curry.'

'But?'

'You'd rather have lasagne and chips in a pub.'

They both laughed.

'What's my guilty pleasure?'

'Wham! Obviously,' Sarah replied. 'What's mine?'

'All Saints,' Ruth giggled. 'But mainly because you really fancy the pants off them.'

Ruth stood up. It was as if some time machine had just sucked the last seven years away.

Sarah began to cough.

'Want some water?' Ruth asked, reaching over to the bedside table and pouring it before she had a chance to answer. 'Here you go.'

Taking a sip, Sarah sat back again and looked at her. 'Maybe we really are here.'

'I actually think we are,' Ruth laughed with a shake of her head. 'I think they're going to throw me out of here in a minute.'

Sarah reached out and took Ruth's hand. Her eyes were now full of tears and her expression had changed from joy to pain.

'I'm sorry,' Sarah whispered. 'I'm so, so sorry ...'

Ruth reached over touched Sarah's cheek with the side of her thumb. 'Hey, none of that matters at the moment. You just need to get some rest, okay?'

The door to the room opened quietly and the nurse came in and smiled.

It was time to go.

CHAPTER 6

Ruth watched the last moments of light fading over the Paris skyline from where she was sitting on the steps of the Basilique du Sacré-Cœur, the huge Roman Catholic church that stood at the summit of Montmartre, the highest point in the city. Even though she wasn't religious, it felt somehow poignant to be sitting at the foot of a church on the day that Sarah had been returned to her. Her relationship with whatever higher power she believed existed in the universe had been a fraught and troublesome one. It had fluctuated from enraged rants about her certainty that there could be no God in a place that had allowed Sarah to disappear without a trace, to focussed prayers for her to be safe and well.

Lighting up a cigarette, Ruth tried to take stock of what had been an extraordinary day. A steady stream of tourists came up the steps. A teenage Asian couple sat ten or so steps down from her holding hands. He was teasing her, carefully brushing hair from her face and kissing her. Her giggle was infectious.

At the top of the steps to her left, an African man was trying to sell golden mini-statues of the Eiffel Tower that were laid out in neat rows on a black cloth on the floor. A mother and her young daughter came past holding hands. They were wearing identical skinny jeans and bright pink trainers.

As Ruth blew out a long plume of smoke she looked at the ornate iron lampposts that wouldn't have looked out of place on the set of *Mary Poppins*.

I found her. I actually found her and I've seen her. How is that possible?

She made a sound like an incredulous laugh in her throat as if it was a ridiculous notion. The pain of Sarah's disappearance, and the anguish of not knowing what had happened, had become the norm over the last seven years.

Shouldn't I be dancing around or popping Champagne corks? she wondered to herself.

If she was honest, she didn't know how to feel or how to process it. She felt numb. There were so many questions she needed Sarah to answer. Looking over at a couple who were in each other's arms and looking out at the skyline, she just didn't know what would happen between her and Sarah. Could they really go back to being together after all that had happened?

Just focus on the basic facts, Ruth, she told herself. *Sarah is alive. You've seen her, you've spoken to her, and you've held her hand. Don't try to begin to think about what is going to happen next.*

Her train of thought was broken by her phone ringing. It was Ella, her daughter. She had left her a very vague message about half an hour earlier.

'Mum?' Ella enquired in an urgent tone.

'I've seen her.' Ruth swallowed as tears filled her eyes.

'What?'

'I saw Sarah. I sat by her bed, I spoke to her, and I held her hand.' Ruth's voice broke with emotion.

There was a long silence and then she heard a sniff. Ella was crying.

'Ella?' she asked.

'Yes, sorry, I ...' Ella sounded totally overwhelmed. 'I can't believe it's true.'

'Neither can I, darling,' Ruth said, realising that the very process of talking to her daughter was making it now feel very real and even more emotional.

'I'll get a plane out there tomorrow. Where are you staying, Mum?'

'No, no,' Ruth protested. 'I really think it's best I'm out here on my own to start with.'

'But I don't want you to be on your own.' Ella sounded a little hurt.

'Darling, of course I would love you to be over here,' Ruth tried to explain, 'but I need some time to talk to Sarah. And I've got to talk to the police and authorities out here. There will be paperwork and statements.'

'Yes, yes, it was a silly idea,' Ella murmured quietly.

'It wasn't a silly idea,' Ruth said. 'I love you so much. And you're the one person who I would want with me here right now, but it's not practical.'

There were a few seconds of silence.

'Is she going to be okay?' Ella asked.

'Yes, I think so,' Ruth replied. 'As far as they know, she's going to make a full recovery.'

'Are you bringing her back to Wales, then?'

'We haven't got that far yet, darling,' Ruth said ruefully. Ella might have been in her early 20s, but she could still have moments of sounding naïve.

'Can you send her my love?'

'Of course.'

Then a few more seconds of silence.

'It's so weird, isn't it Mum?' Ella whispered.

'Yes, it is,' she admitted. 'I can't seem to get my head around it.'

'Are you going to be all right?'

'I'm going to be fine. Don't worry.'

'Will you call me in the morning?' Ella asked.

Ruth got up from the steps. Her back and legs were still sore from earlier. 'Of course.'

'I love you, Mum.'

'I love you too darling. I'll talk to you in the morning. Sleep well.'

Ruth ended the call and winced as she began to walk down the steps away from the Basilique and towards her hotel a few minutes away.

The hotel room door buzzed as Ruth slotted the key card in and out of the lock. She opened the heavy door, put the card into the slot on the wall to activate the lights, and went in. It smelled clean and fresh. All she wanted was to have a hot bath, maybe something to eat and drink from room service, and crawl into bed.

She was staying at the Terrass Hotel in Montmartre at the junction of rue Joseph de Maistre with rue Caulaincourt. The classic early 20th century nine-floor building had been recently renovated to give a smart and functional contemporary feel. Ruth's room was small and she wasn't sure about its *chic* red and black design. It looked like something from the 80s she thought, but she didn't have the wherewithal to really care.

She unzipped her navy jacket, took it off, and tossed it onto a nearby armchair. Then she noticed that the material had split right in the middle at the back where the bullet had hit her bulletproof vest. With all the commotion around Sarah, she had virtually forgotten that she had been shot and almost blown up eight hours earlier. Gazing at the split material, it struck her that without the bulletproof vest she would now be dead.

I could do with the next few months being very boring and uneventful, she thought to herself, even though she knew that was unlikely.

She finished undressing and put on the complimentary white robe which was big and soft. She stepped into the bathroom and turned on the taps to run herself a bath. Everything about the bathroom was modern and sleek. The white painted brickwork, the black and white mosaic floor and the Hollywood bulb lights that went around the mirror.

As the bath was filling, she went back into the room, took the remote control and clicked on the flat screen television that was mounted on the wall. As she surfed through the channels, she stopped at TF1. There was aerial footage of the Forêt de Sénart, followed by footage of the farmhouse which had been severely damaged by the explosion and fire. A red banner running across the bottom of the screen read *DERNIÈRES NOUVELLES*. She assumed it meant *Breaking News* or something similar. The news anchor was speaking over the footage and she found it frustrating that she couldn't understand any of it.

Going back into the bathroom, she began to turn off the taps. Swishing the water, she realised it was a few degrees too hot. She decided to look through the room service menu. She wasn't particularly hungry but a large glass of red wine wasn't a bad idea. Casting her eye over to the sink, she noticed that something wasn't quite right.

Despite her general untidyness, Ruth had a habit of laying out her toothbrush, toothpaste, deodorant and moisturiser in the same order when she arrived at a hotel. Although she had only been in the room for a few minutes earlier in the day, she had put them in the order that she was going to use them, as she always did. Except they weren't in that order any more.

Am I losing the plot? she wondered. Given how preoccupied she had been when arriving at the hotel, maybe she had just forgotten to follow her routine.

However, her instincts as a copper made her go back into her room and look around.

Her mobile phone buzzed where she had left it on the bedside table. It was Nick, her work colleague and friend back in Wales. She wondered if it was work or personal. If she was to guess, it would be Nick checking to see if she was okay.

She pressed the answer button. 'Nick?'

'I'm watching the BBC news. Are you okay?' he asked, his voice full of concern.

She hadn't even thought that he knew where she was, or why she had travelled to Paris.

'Oh God, I'm sorry,' she apologised. 'I'm fine. Really.'

'Did you find Sarah?' he asked.

She waited a few seconds to compose herself before replying.

'Yes, I did.'

'Jesus. Is she okay?' Nick asked, sounding shocked.

'She's in hospital but she's going to make a full recovery. She just needs to rest.'

'Did you speak to her?'

'Yes.'

There was a brief silence. Nick knew all about what had happened with Sarah and her disappearance.

'Bloody hell, Ruth!' he exclaimed. 'What was that like?'

'Erm, amazing, surreal, strange ... I don't know.'

Opening the wardrobe, she looked down at her small, navy blue trolley case.

It's been moved, she thought.

She pulled it out from the wardrobe, placed it on the bed, and opened it.

'What happens now?'

'I'm going back to the hospital tomorrow,' she said as she looked at her things that lay in her case.

Someone has been through my bloody case, she thought.

'And then what?' he asked.

'I just don't know.' Ruth took the small work briefcase from the bedside table where she had put it when she had first arrived and checked in. 'I want to make sure Sarah's okay.'

'Of course.'

'After that, I've no idea. I'm just trying to get my head around it.' Ruth looked at the documents and photos connected to Sarah's case that she had brought from the UK with her. 'I won't be back in CID until next week though.'

'Take your time. This is such a big thing for you.'

'Yeah, it really is.' Ruth was distracted. There was no doubt in her mind. Someone had been in her briefcase and gone through all the documents. She was an experienced detective with an acute eye for detail.

'I wish there was something I could do to help. Is there anything you need?'

'Hot bath, wine and sleep,' she sighed.

'Sounds like a plan. I'll leave you to it then, eh?'

'Yeah. How are the girls?'

'Fine. We're all fine,' he replied. 'We just want to make sure you're okay.'

'It'll work out somehow. I'll send you an update tomorrow, okay?'

'That would be great.'

'Nick?'

'Yeah?'

'Thanks.'

'No problem.'

The call ended.

Walking over to the hotel phone beside the bed, Ruth was now a little spooked that someone had been into the room and been through her things. She pressed the button marked *0*.

A voice in a thick French accent answered, 'Reception?'

'Hi, I'm in Room 14. I checked in earlier today.'

'Yes, madame.'

'Can you tell me if anyone has been in my room today while I was out?' she asked.

'Let me just check that for you, madame,' the receptionist replied. 'No, madame. No one has been into your room today. Is there anything I can help you with?'

'No, no, it's fine,' Ruth reassured him.

'Okay. Goodnight, madame.'

'Yes, thank you. Goodnight.' Ruth hung up the phone.

What the hell is going on?

CHAPTER 7

Rolling over onto her back, Ruth felt the blinding pain between her shoulder blades again. Her sleep had been fitful. Not only did she have bruises scattered all over her body, but she had to deal with the emotional turmoil of finding and speaking to Sarah.

With some effort, she manoeuvred herself up against the pillows, grabbed the television remote, and searched the channels. She had so many things racing around her head, vying for her attention.

What is Sarah going to reveal when we start to unpick the seven years of her disappearance? How am I going to deal with all that?

Ruth also wondered if the police raid had brought them any closer to arresting Patrice Le Bon and Sergei Saratov. As she glanced at her briefcase, she remembered that someone had been into her room the previous day and gone through her things. What was that all about?

She lifted the briefcase from the bedside table and opened it on her lap, checking carefully to make sure that everything was still there. There were documents pertaining to Jamie Parsons, Jurgen Kessler and the Secret Garden parties, and a large photo of Patrice Le Bon standing beside the River Seine with some of his cronies.

Her attention was drawn to the television as BBC News 24 appeared on the screen. A reporter was talking to the camera with the farmhouse at Forêt de Sénart behind him.

'It was mid-afternoon when this seemingly peaceful French farm became a bloody battleground. Members of the elite French firearms unit, RAID, entered this farmhouse behind me to rescue up to a dozen sex workers who were being held against their will. In the resulting firefight, one of the captors was shot dead and two were seriously wounded. The police operation is believed to have been part of an ongoing investigation into international human trafficking, and comes on the heels of several failed raids in the French capital itself. Martin Bruce has more.'

As she leaned back a little against the pillows, a photograph appeared on the screen, as a voice-over continued. 'The French police's investigation into human trafficking centres on two men - Russian billionaire Sergie Saratov, who was at the centre of a scandal involving sex workers at his luxury hotels in Switzerland, and Patrice Le Bon, a wealthy French businessmen with political ambitions. There are many commentators who believe that the scandal involving the trafficking of sex workers into France will have ramifications into the upper eschelons of French society and the French government itself.'

Throwing back the duvet, Ruth's mind now turned to getting showered, dressed, and seeing Sarah.

Ruth walked along the ground floor of the hospital drinking the coffee she had bought from a stall near the entrance. She had the briefcase of documents with her, just in case.

There was a central atrium in the hospital with palm trees, neat bushes and benches. The glass of the outside walls and roof let in so much light that she felt like she was almost walking through some modern park.

She stepped into a lift and pressed the button for the USI on the sixth floor. Just as the doors began to close, a woman in her 50s approached and entered. She was attractive, and was wearing a stylish navy business suit.

'Detective Inspector Hunter?' she asked, as the doors closed silently behind her.

'Yes?' Ruth answered uncertainly. She had no idea who this woman was.

'Agent Camille Moreau. I am with the DGSE.' she informed her. It stood for the Direction Générale de la Sécurité Extérieure which was the French Security Service.

Ruth nodded. 'I know the DGSE.'

'I need to talk to you about your friend Sarah Goddard, and also about this investigation. I think you know quite a lot about it.'

Moreau said this in a way that made Ruth feel uncomfortable. Her tone almost implied that Ruth knew more than she should. Maybe she was being paranoid? But then she thought about the fact that someone had been through her personal things, and looked at all the notes on the case that she had collected in the last seven years. It wouldn't be beyond the realms of possibility that the French Security Service had been into her room to check out what she knew.

'I'm on my way to see Sarah now,' Ruth said a little sharply. She didn't have the time or the inclination to run through all that she knew with a stranger. Her concern was to see Sarah and check that she was okay.

'Yes,' Moreau nodded as the lift arrived at the sixth floor. 'I am speaking to her today along with the other women that were rescued.'

As they stepped out of the lift Ruth said, 'Can we speak later? I'm going to be in the hospital all day. I'd like to go and see Sarah right now.'

'Yes, of course. I will come and find you. There is no particular hurry.' Moreau then thought for a moment and looked at her watch. 'Maybe you could meet me in the café on the ground floor at twelve?'

'Okay, no problem,' Ruth replied as she watched Moreau getting back into the lift. There was something about their encounter that had made her feel uneasy.

After pressing the buzzer outside the USI, a nurse she recognised from the previous evening approached and opened the sliding glass so Ruth could enter. The nurse was mixed race and had cornrows under her white cap. Her large eyes were brown and her complexion was flawless.

'Bonjour madame,' she murmured gently with a smile. 'Ta amie va beaucoup mieus ce matin.'

Ruth didn't know exactly what that meant. She thought *ce matin* was *this morning*, and the tone of her voice had been positive, so she assumed there was little to worry about.

As they made their way across the USI towards the corner room where she had seen Sarah the night before, Ruth noticed a strong smell of hospital food and coffee.

The nurse opened the door gently, gave Ruth a smile and left. As she went in, Sarah turned and looked at her.

'How are you?' Ruth asked in a virtual whisper.

'Fine.' Sarah's face broke into a smile. 'They gave me some kind of drug to make me sleep and that did the trick.'

'Always been a bit of a druggie,' Ruth quipped as she went over and sat down on the chair next to the bed.

'That's rich coming from you.' Sarah laughed and then winced. 'Ow, it really hurts to laugh.'

'I didn't know what to bring you. You don't like grapes. But there's a few shops on the ground floor, so I can go and get anything you ...'

'I need to tell you what happened,' Sarah interrupted. It was clear that she was very preoccupied.

'It's fine.' Ruth reached over and touched her hand. 'I just want you to get better. Then we can do all that.'

Sarah shook her head. 'No, Ruth.' The smile had now gone. 'I have to tell you. It's driving me mad. I don't think I can settle until we talk.'

Ruth nodded slowly and rubbed her face. She could see that Sarah was agitated, but this was going to be difficult, uncomfortable and painful. 'Okay ... I guess I'm trying to put off doing this because I'm scared of what you're going to tell me.'

'I know. But we can't pretend it's going to go away. And there's stuff you have to know right now.'

'Okay.' Ruth leaned back in her chair. 'You're right.'

'What do you know?' Sarah asked.

'Christ, where do I start, Sarah?' Ruth took a breath, shook her head and held back the tears. 'I just want to know why? Why did you do that to me?'

There were a few seconds of tense silence.

Sarah's eyes filled with tears as she asked, 'Do you know about Jamie Parsons?'

Ruth nodded as she wiped her face and blew out her cheeks. 'Yes. I know you had an affair.'

Sarah looked at her. 'I'm so sorry,' she whispered.

'Why did you?'

'I don't know. I can hardly remember.' Sarah shook her head slowly. 'You always worked such long hours but it seemed as if I just never saw you. And when you did get home, you'd have a glass of wine and fall asleep. We didn't do anything together. You even cancelled Glastonbury that summer.'

'You had an affair because we didn't go to Glastonbury?' Ruth's voice was forceful, her tone abrupt, but she knew that's not what Sarah meant.

'No! But we missed The Rolling Stones and I was angry with you.'

Ruth folded her arms across her chest and leaned forward. 'So, you just decided to have an affair with some terrible, stuck up, rich, entitled twat?'

Sarah shrugged. 'Yeah, Jamie was a twat. But he was an exciting twat and well connected and ...'

'And rich?'

'Yeah, he was rich,' Sarah admitted. 'I'm not going to say that wasn't part of the attraction.'

'You went to the Secret Garden parties with him, didn't you?'

'Oh God!' Sarah's eyes widened. 'You know about that?'

'Of course, I do!' Ruth snapped. 'I was a bloody detective looking for my partner. I spent every spare minute trying to find you. Have you any idea what that was like?'

Sarah shifted awkwardly in the bed and shook her head almost imperceptibly. 'No, I don't. And I don't expect you to ever forgive me for that.'

Ruth tried to put a lid on the hurt and anger she was feeling. 'How does any of what you told me explain what happened on November 5th?'

Sarah gave her a grave look and whispered, 'I saw something that I wasn't meant to see.'

'What?' Ruth asked, her eyebrows raised in question.

Sarah stopped for a few seconds and stared into space, clearly recalling what had happened.

Ruth prompted her. 'What did you see?'

'I did some coke in one of the en suites at the Secret Garden,' she explained. 'Before I could get out, I heard some kind of argument. Then there was a scream and some shouting. I opened the door slightly to have a look. A man was on top of this girl in the bedroom. She couldn't have been more than sixteen ...' Sarah's voice broke a little with the emotion of recounting what she had seen.

'Go on,' Ruth murmured quietly.

'I ... I thought he was raping this girl. I was about to go and stop him ... but then I realised she wasn't making any sound or moving. The man had his right hand around her throat ... and ...'

'What?'

Sarah looked at her as her eyes filled with tears again.

Ruth was horrified. 'Was she dead?'

'Yes.' Sarah nodded. 'He must have strangled her.'

'Jesus,' Ruth gasped.

'I didn't know what to do,' Sarah said, fighting the tremor in her voice. 'And then the room door opened and four men came in.'

'You saw them?'

'Yes.' Sarah blinked away the tears. 'It was Jamie Parsons, his friend Jurgen Kessler, Patrice Le Bon and Sergie Saratov. Saratov is this Russian billionaire ...'

Ruth interrupted her. 'It's all right. I know who all of them are.'

Sarah's eyes widened. 'Even Jurgen Kessler?'

'Yes,' Ruth replied, although it wasn't the time to explain how. 'What happened next?'

'When they realised the man had killed her, they started to argue about what they were going to do about it. They agreed that it had to be covered up and they needed to get rid of the girl's body. The man who killed her was crying ...'

'Did you get to see him?'

Sarah's expression changed to one of fear.

'Who was he?'

After hesitating for a few seconds she whispered, 'David Weaver.'

Ruth looked at her in disbelief. 'Lord Weaver?'

Sarah nodded.

Lord David Weaver was a life peer who had served as both Foreign Secretary and Chief Whip in the late 1980s. He was a very visible member of the House of Lords, often photographed with the great and the good, the rich and the famous. His wife Olivia moved in social circles with lesser members of the Royal Family.

'Bloody hell, Sarah!' Ruth exclaimed. What she had seen was both horrendous and shocking.

'I was waiting for them all to go but I knew they weren't going to leave that poor girl there. I must have knocked the lock with my hand or something because Jamie heard a noise and came over. He opened the door fully and saw me standing there. Then all hell broke loose.'

'Not surprising! You'd just witnessed a peer of the realm murdering a teenage girl.'

'After they had talked about what to do with me, Jamie ushered me away to another room. I thought they were going to kill me too.' Sarah's eyes filled with tears. 'He said the only way for me to stay alive was to disappear. He would arrange for it to happen but I couldn't tell anyone. He told me that Saratov wanted me to be killed and got rid of, so this was my only option. Three days later, I got on that train to Victoria and met Jurgen Kessler. We got off at Vauxhall. A car whizzed me over to the heliport at Battersea, and a helicopter took us across the channel to some place in France.'

Running her hands through her hair, Ruth tried to take in what Sarah had just told her. All the pieces of information now fitted together.

Ruth cleared her throat to mask the choke in her voice. 'Oh my God, Sarah! I can't believe all that happened to you.'

Sarah sobbed. 'I'm so, so sorry. They warned me if I tried to tell you or contact you, they would kill me and then kill you.'

They hugged and Ruth felt Sarah's body shaking as she wept.

Taking her face in her hands, Ruth kissed Sarah's wet cheeks. 'I can't believe you've been living with that for seven years.'

'I've got used to it ...' she admitted as she blinked away the tears and took Ruth's hand in hers, '... but I'm scared.'

'Why are you scared now?'

'What if they find out I'm here?' she asked nervously.

'You think you're in danger in here?'

'Of course.' Sarah's breathing was getting shallow. 'Patrice Le Bon knew exactly where we all were. He knew who I was.'

Ruth squeezed her hand, trying to work out what to do next. 'It's okay. I'm here for starters.'

'You won't be able to stop them,' Sarah warned. 'Le Bon has got friends everywhere in Paris. He supplies escorts to government ministers, the Deputy Chief of Police, film stars, you name it.'

Ruth was beginning to feel very uncomfortable. 'You're going to have to go on record about what you saw that night ... and David Weaver.'

Sarah shook her head. She looked terrified. 'I can't do that.'

'Of course you can.'

'Don't you get it? These men have enough power and money to get to anyone, anywhere. They supply escorts and teenage girls to the richest, most powerful men in the world. They're not going to allow me to testify that I saw all those men and Lord David Weaver arguing about what to do with the dead body of a teenage girl,' Sarah stammered, starting to hyperventilate.

Ruth placed her hands on her shoulders. 'Hey, you've got to calm down.'

'They're going to kill both of us,' Sarah whimpered. She was bordering on hysterical.

'No, they're not!' Ruth snapped firmly, and looked directly in her eyes. 'I'm not going to let them do that. They've already robbed you and me of the last seven years.'

'What are we going to do then?' Sarah asked. She was now visibly shaking.

'They don't know you're here,' Ruth reassured her. 'At the moment, you're listed as a Sophie Collins. You're safe in here for a while.'

Sarah nodded as she began to calm down. 'Okay.'

'I'm not going to let anything happen to you. Understand?'

'Yeah, I know.' Sarah closed her eyes for a moment and tried to compose herself.

'But to be on the safe side, I'll talk to the doctors and see if we can get you moved. At the moment, only a handful of people know that you're here, okay?'

'Okay,' Sarah sighed, nodding again. Her breathing had started to regulate but she started to cough.

Ruth turned to the bedside cabinet and picked up a jug and cup. 'Let me get you some water.'

'Thanks.'

As Ruth turned back to hand it to her, she knocked a small orange container of pills onto the floor. She bent down and picked it up, glancing at the label as she placed it back on the table. It read – *PubChem C21H27NO Methadone 10mgs.*

She frowned and looked at Sarah. 'Methadone?'

Sarah didn't say anything.

Ruth reached down and pulled up the sleeve on her hospital gown. Sarah didn't resist but she looked away. Her right forearm bore the telltale injection marks of an intravenous heroin addict. As a police officer, Ruth had seen it many times before.

She took Sarah's hand. 'How long?'

'Three years,' she whispered.

'Injecting?'

Sarah shook her head. 'No. I smoked it for the first two years, but then the effects eventually wore off ... It was the only way to cope with it, I'm sorry.'

Ruth squeezed her hand. 'Hey, it's okay. You did what you had to do to survive. We can get you better. Okay?'

Sarah nodded. 'Yes. Thank you.'

'And you're in the best place so you can safely detox for a few days.'

'I know, but I'm just so ashamed.'

Ruth smiled at her. 'Don't be. None of this is your fault.'

They sat in silence for a few seconds.

'How's Ella?' Sarah asked.

'She's fine,' Ruth replied. 'More than fine. She's amazing. She asked me to say hello and that she can't wait to see you.'

'Have you got a photo? I bet she's changed loads.'

Taking out her phone, Ruth found a recent photo of her daughter and showed it to Sarah.

'Oh wow, she's beautiful!'

'Thanks. She's so grown up and together.'

'Where does she get that from?' Sarah joked.

'Hey!' Ruth smiled. 'And the best thing is that she doesn't resemble her father in a any way.

They laughed.

Ruth looked down at the phone again and saw there was no signal. She could do with talking to Oliver Trelford for starters. She wasn't sure how much she could trust the police in Paris. Then maybe a phone call to Stephen Flaherty, her missing persons liaison officer at the Met in London.

Ruth gestured to her phone, then looked at her watch. It was 10.30am. 'Listen, I need to make a couple of phone calls.

I'll be back in five minutes. I'll go downstairs to the shop. What do you want?'

'Full fat coke,' Sarah replied. Her tear-stained face broke into a half smile.

'Full fat coke. Salt and vinegar crisps?' Ruth asked. It had been their classic hangover cure.

'Yes please ... I'm so sorry I've put you through all this.'

'Look, maybe I did take you for granted back then,' Ruth admitted. 'And maybe I can understand how your head might have been turned by someone like Jamie Parsons. But what you saw happen to that girl isn't your fault, okay?'

'I never stopped loving you, you know that?'

'I know,' Ruth replied and smiled. 'Now I'm going to be gone for fifteen minutes, twenty max. Don't get into any trouble.'

Sarah gestured to the drips in her arms and the monitors. 'Chance would be a fine thing.'

CHAPTER 8

The lift doors opened on the ground floor and Ruth got out and turned left towards a large coffee shop, *Le Café au Lait*, which was next to a newsagents. A couple who looked worried sat holding hands by a rectangular pool of water that had gentle water fountains in a symmetrical line down its centre. To her right, there was a series of café-style tables with navy umbrellas to shield customers from the intense light that was shining down through the glass roof. Waiters shuffled back and forth with cups of coffee, croissants and pastries. Huge pots of bright green foliage and shrubs had been placed at regular intervals to create natural-looking breaks between the tables. The hospital had essentially recreated a pristine Parisienne street at its centre. Ruth thought that the ageing Victorian hospitals of London and North Wales could learn a thing or two from what had been achieved in the Hôpital Européen Georges-Pompidou.

She now had her mobile phone clamped to her ear while she waited for Stephen Flaherty to answer her call.

'Come on, come on,' she growled as she weaved past a huddle of nurses coming the other way.

As she reached *Le Café au Lait,* she had the distinct impression that someone was following her. Spinning around, she caught sight of a man in a bandana and sunglasses. He stopped and pretended to look at a floor map of the hospital.

Nice try, mate, she thought. *I'm 99% certain he's following me, but why?*

'Stephen Flaherty,' said a voice that she recognised.

Stephen, from London's Met Police Missing Persons Unit, had been assigned to investigate Sarah's disappearance back in November 2013. Ever since then, he and Ruth had kept in regular contact. In the early years, he had often rung to sadly tell her that there was no news. In fact, after the first few years, there was part of Ruth that knew the odds of finding Sarah alive were a million to one. The most likely scenario was that she had been abducted from the train by someone who subsequently murdered her and disposed of her body. As a detective, Ruth knew more than most people that Sarah was never going to be found alive. As far as anyone knew, she'd had no reason to leave. There were no money worries, she was happy in her job, and on the surface she was content sharing her life with Ruth in their flat in Crystal Palace. Ruth could never have guessed what had really happened to her. In fact it still felt so unreal. Sarah had witnessed a murder, and it was taking Ruth some time to process the events of seven years ago.

She cleared her throat and said, 'Stephen, it's Ruth. I'm at the hospital with Sarah.'

'That's incredible!' He sounded full of joy. 'How is she?'

'Nasty bang to the head but she's going to be okay. At the moment, I've got her here under a false name. But we do have a problem.'

'Really? Go on.'

'In November 2013, Sarah witnessed a peer of the British realm murder a teenage girl at a Secret Garden sex party.'

'What? Jesus!' he said with an incredulous gasp.

'There were some very powerful people involved in covering it up. That's why Sarah disappeared. She was the only witness and was told that if she didn't do as she was told, both she and I were to be killed. I can't tell you any more than that over the phone.'

'Okay, I understand,' he murmured quietly. 'I can't pretend that I'm not completely shocked.'

'Yes, it's horrendous. The problem we have is that I have no idea how safe Sarah is here. She seems to think that the people who took her and kept her all this time have contacts everywhere, especially in Paris. She told me that the Deputy Chief of Police here in Paris was a client of Global Escorts.'

'Right. We need to get her into some kind of witness protection and bring her back onto UK soil.'

'At the moment, she's too afraid to even contemplate testifying to what she saw, but I think I can persuade her once the dust has settled.'

'Do you think you can trust the Paris Police at all?' he asked.

'I just don't know,' Ruth admitted. If she was honest, she just didn't know who to trust.

'Your best bet would be your UK Interpol liaison then,' Stephen suggested.

'You're right. His name is Oliver Trelford. He seems like a decent bloke.'

'Interpol is a completely independent law enforcement agency. It's politically neutral. He should be your first port of call.'

'Makes sense.'

'Let me make some phone calls Ruth. It might be that we send officers over from the Met to escort you and Sarah home. Leave it with me, okay?'

The call ended.

Ruth's head was a whirring muddle. She needed to get hold of Trelford and keep both the Paris Police and Agent Moreau from the DGSE at arms length until she heard back from Stephen. Her instinct was that it was better to trust those on the UK side than those in Paris.

Marching into the café, she looked around and spotted a large upright fridge full of soft drinks.

What am I getting? Two full fat cokes, she said to herself. She was finding it difficult to concentrate on anything. She reached in and picked up two cokes.

'Best cure for a hangover, I find,' said a voice. It was Agent Moreau.

'What's that?' Ruth asked.

'Proper Coca-Cola.' Moreau gestured to the cans she was holding. 'Plenty of sugar and caffeine.'

Ruth smiled. She wasn't quite sure what to make of her. 'Yes, I'm running on empty so ...'

Moreau looked puzzled. 'What is *running on empty*?'

'I'm just very tired, that's all,' Ruth explained, and then looked at her watch. It was 10.55am. She needed to get back to Sarah.

'I have another one of the women from the farmhouse to talk to,' Moreau said, 'but we can still meet back here at twelve?'

Ruth smiled and nodded. 'Yes, of course. That's fine.'

Moreau strode away towards the lifts and Ruth watched her go. She quite fancied her.

To the left of the fridge was a large window that looked out over the vast hospital car park. She spotted something in the car park out of the corner of her eye.

A figure standing smoking by a car.

It was Vernier.

Maybe he had come to visit Sarah today and take a statement? Ruth would stall him by telling him that she wasn't up to answering any questions for a day or two. That would allow Stephen to set things up from the UK.

A figure joined Vernier by the car. A man in a long dark overcoat. She assumed he was another police officer.

Going to the till, Ruth grabbed two packets of crisps and paid for them along with the two cans in her hand. They were so cold that it was beginning to become uncomfortable just holding them. She and Sarah agreed that full fat coke could never be too cold. It just wasn't possible.

As she headed for the exit, Ruth couldn't help but walk over to another window and look out over the car park again. It was just the instinctive curiosity of a detective.

Vernier and the man were still smoking and talking intensely. Whatever they were talking about, they both seemed fractious and agitated.

As the man turned, she saw his face. She thought she recognised him from somewhere but couldn't remember where. His white hair was shoulder length, and his face very pale - both of which were in stark contrast to his dark coat.

As she watched, a black BMW 4x4 with blacked out windows pulled up beside them. They got in quickly and the car sped away.

As she headed out of the café, there was something about the man's appearance that had made her feel very uneasy. She didn't know what it was, but she needed to get back to Sarah with the coke and crisps.

As the doors to the lift opened on the sixth floor, Ruth looked out to see Trelford waiting for her. He smiled and gave her an uncertain wave.

'I saw you coming up, so I thought I'd wait for you,' he explained pointing to the glass lifts and lift shaft that meant you could see everyone going up and down. 'How's Sarah?'

He had that slight social awkwardness that she had found in many public school educated men, but she liked Trelford. Her instincts told her that he was one of the good guys.

'She's fine.' Ruth gestured towards the USI. Something about what she had seen in the car park had spooked her and she was keen to get back to Sarah. 'Bumps and bruises, but that's about it.'

'Good, good. Glad to hear it,' Trelford chirped brightly as they marched towards the door.

'There is something I'm going to need your help with,' Ruth requested as they reached the unit.

'That's what I'm here for.'

He sounds very relaxed. Christ, wait until I tell him what I actually need help with!

Ruth pressed the buzzer and a nurse that she didn't recognise came over and let them in.

'To say that what I'm going to tell you is shocking would be an understatement,' Ruth warned him as they strode across the unit.

He shrugged. 'I work for Interpol. I once spent a ten-hour car drive handcuffed to the most dangerous Islamic terrorist on the planet at the time.'

Yes, well this is going to blow your mind!

They arrived at the corner room where Sarah had been, only to see that her bed had been made and was now empty.

Ruth panicked. 'What the hell is going on?' she snapped, looking at Trelford.

The nurse began to speak in French as Ruth's heart started to race.

'What's she saying?' Ruth asked anxiously and then glared at the nurse. 'Where is she?'

'It's okay.' Trelford put a reassuring hand on her shoulder.

'It's not okay! Where the bloody hell is she?'

'They just needed to use this bed. They've moved Sarah to another ward, that's all. She didn't need to be in here.'

Ruth blew out her cheeks with relief. 'Sorry. I'm just a bit jumpy.'

'I can see that. But it's a positive thing. It means that she's recovering well.'

'I know. Sorry.' Ruth looked at the nurse with an apologetic expression. 'Pardon, madame.' Can she tell us which ward she is on?' she asked Trelford.

He spoke to the nurse in French and then looked at Ruth. 'It's the far ward on the third floor.'

They made their way out of the USI and headed for the lifts. She was glad that Trelford was there as a reassuring presence.

'Sorry for snapping,' she said.

'Hey, don't worry. If I'd been through what you've been through in the last twenty four hours, I'd be snapping too,' he joked.

'How long have you been in Paris, Oliver?' she asked as she pressed the button to summon the ultra-modern glass lift.

'Over ten years now.'

'And you like it?'

'Sometimes,' he replied with a shrug. 'We do a lot of surveillance, and you know what that's like.'

The doors to the lift opened and they got in. He pressed the button for the third floor.

'Boring as hell.'

'But I'm a linguist, so I get a lot of translation stuff which is more my thing.'

'How many languages do you speak?' she asked as the lift descended and she looked out of the glass at the enormous central atrium.

The Glasshouse in Kew Gardens. That's what it reminds me of, she thought to herself.

'All European.'

'Fluent?'

'Not all. French, Spanish, Italian, German, Russian,' he said. 'My speciality is Arabic though.'

Ruth looked at him. 'Which is why you're in Paris.'

'Exactly.'

There had been a long history of Arabic immigration into the city from the 60s onwards, especially from the French-speaking colonies of North Africa, as well as Senegal, the Ivory Coast and Cameroon.

'Oxbridge then?'

'Of course,' he admitted. 'Is it that obvious?'

Ruth laughed, 'Yes.'

'My boyfriend also lives in Paris so ...'

'Did you meet here?' Ruth asked. For some reason, she was surprised at his openness.

'Yes.' Trelford smiled. 'Our eyes met over a cheese baguette when we were both doing a course at the Sorbonne.'

Ruth gave a half laugh. 'That is very romantic. What's his name?'

'Ousmane.'

Ruth looked confused. It wasn't a French-sounding name.

'He's orginally from the Ivory Coast,' Trelford clarified.

'And you live together?' Ruth paused and raised a hand as if to fend off the answer. 'Sorry, I feel like I'm giving you the third degree here.'

'No, it's fine. It's nice that you ask. We have a lovely apartment looking over the Seine.'

'That sounds very romantic.'

'Sometimes.' Trelford gave her a wry smile. 'You know what it's like.'

Ruth nodded. 'Yeah, all too well.'

As they came out of the lift on the third floor, the man wearing the bandana and sunglasses was sitting on a bench on the other side of the corridor. Even though he was talking on his mobile phone, he clearly looked over at her.

'Friend of yours?' Trelford asked.

'No,' Ruth replied. 'I just keep seeing him everywhere I go in this hospital.'

'You think he's following you?'

'I'm not sure.'

They continued the long walk down the glass-flanked corridors which were bright and air conditioned.

Ruth glanced back over her shoulder but the bandana man was nowhere to be seen. Maybe she was just being paranoid.

'This hospital is enormous,' she groaned after another minute walking. 'I'm out of breath.'

'Don't worry,' Trelford pointed to a ward on the right, 'this is it.'

Even though she felt a little uneasy, Ruth was certain that moving Sarah from the USI to a day ward while she recovered made perfect sense.

Trelford went over to the nurses' station and explained why they were there and that they were looking for a patient called *Sophie Collins*.

After a long discussion, Trelford came over with a bewildered look on his face.

'What's wrong?' Ruth asked. His expression immediately concerned her.

Trelford frowned. 'I don't understand.'

'What's going on, Oliver? You're starting to scare me.'

'Sarah was here.'

'So where is she now?' she demanded.

'She discharged herself about ten minutes ago.'

'What?' Ruth exclaimed loudly. 'No, that's just not possible!'

'The sister in charge said that a man came to talk to Sarah. He had a wheelchair with him and claimed that he was her uncle. He talked to Sarah, and then he helped her sign the French patient self-discharge form. Then they left together, with Sarah in the wheelchair.'

'Didn't anyone think to stop them!' Ruth thundered to no one in particular.

Oh my God! This cannot be happening!

Without thinking, Ruth turned and sprinted back towards the lifts. She weaved in and out of patients and doctors as she hammered down the corridor. The muscles in her legs began to burn and she sucked in more air.

As she turned each corner, only to see another long corridor in front of her, her anxiety was becoming overwhelming.

I'm not going to lose her again! I won't let that happen!

She arrived at the lift just as the doors were closing. She thrust her hand forwards, forcing them to reopen, much to the annoyance of everyone in there. There wasn't time to worry about that.

As the doors closed, she gasped for a few seconds. Then she spun around as the lift moved slowly downwards. She bent double, trying to get her breath. Frankly, she didn't give a shit about what anyone else thought.

Rushing to the far side of the lift where she could see the ground floor below, she spotted a man wheeling a patient along the central atrium towards the main hospital entrance.

Was that Sarah? It had to be.

For a few seconds, she hammered on the window in the hope of attracting their attention, but it was no use. The people in the lift backed away from her as if she was mad – which at this moment, she was.

The man and Sarah disappeared out of the hospital and out of sight.

No! No!

It was at least another agonising thirty seconds before the lift opened on the ground floor.

Ruth pushed her way out, knocking people to one side. She didn't care.

She sprinted down the central atrium, pumping her arms as she pelted at full speed and headed towards the main entrance.

The huge electronic doors opened as she approached and she ran out into the warm sunshine.

Where are they? Where the fuck are they?

Looking frantically left and right, all she could see was the enormous hospital car park with hundreds of cars.

No! No! This can't be happening! I can't lose them!

Then in the distance, she saw a grey-haired man with a patient in a wheelchair.

'Stop there!' she screamed as she chased after them.

She zig-zagged in and out of the nurses, doctors and patients heading into the hospital.

'Wait there!' she thundered as she ran.

The man seemed to slow a little and looked around as she approached.

'Don't you fucking move another inch!' she yelled as she reached him.

The man, who was well into his 70s, looked scared and held up his hands. 'Mais que se passe-t-il?'

Ruth grabbed the wheelchair and turned it around. 'You're not taking her anywhere!'

To her horror, an old woman in her 70s was looking up at her from the wheelchair and shaking with fear.

'Sorry, sorry,' Ruth mumbled. 'I'm so sorry.'

She stumbled a few steps forward and felt faint. Reaching out, she held onto a handrail and took some deep breaths.

'NO!' she wailed at top of her voice. 'For fuck's sake!'

Sarah was gone.

CHAPTER 9

Two hours had passed since Sarah had been taken from the hospital. Trelford had promised to do everything he could to find out where she had gone, but he warned her that his powers through Interpol were limited.

Ruth was back at La Préfecture de Police in central Paris where she had been the previous day. However, she was in Vernier's dark, cluttered office trying to persuade him that Sarah had not discharged herself from the hospital voluntarily.

Vernier looked over at her across his untidy desk. 'We have no reason to believe that your friend ...'

'Sarah,' she snapped at him. His indifference was really starting to anger her.

'Sarah,' he muttered taking a pen from a grubby looking pot, '... was abducted or kidnapped from the hospital. I have the witness statement from the nurse in front of me. A man came to see her. He said he was her uncle. They spoke. She discharged herself. She didn't shout out or fight. She just left the hospital, as is her right.'

'She was terrified. It's called duress or intimidation.'

Vernier pointed to the witness statement. 'But that is not what the nurse saw.'

'She has been held captive for over seven years!' Ruth shouted. 'Imagine the psychological impact of that.'

'I am sorry, Detective Inspector Hunter,' Vernier grumbled as he sat back in his padded chair, 'but there is nothing to suggest that Sarah was taken by force or against her will from that hospital.'

'Don't be so bloody ridiculous! She's been free from her captors for less than forty eight hours. She's not going to discharge herself and leave the hospital with a strange man when she knows I'm coming back from the café ten minutes later.'

Vernier shrugged. 'He stated he was her uncle.'

'Come on! She doesn't have a bloody *uncle* full stop! She's been held captive and sex-trafficked around Europe for years. This man was one of her captors. She was terrified!'

Vernier took a deep breath. His face showed no emotion. 'I am a police officer. You know my hands are tied unless I can show that a crime has been committed. What am I meant to do?'

Ruth shook her head in despair. 'Use your common sense!' she bellowed. 'How does your instinct as an experienced police officer *not* suggest to you that something here is very wrong? I thought the Paris Police were trying to investigate Global Escorts, sex trafficking into your city, and any connections Patrice Le Bon has to that?'

'Yes. We have an ongoing investigation. And Sarah might prove to be a valuable witness, *if* she agrees to testify against her captors. However, I can't mobilise the whole of the Paris Police force to look for a possible witness who has voluntarily walked out of a hospital. I have no evidence that a crime has been committed. I could lose my job. I don't know you. I don't know Sarah. I don't know what kind of a relationship you have.'

Ruth glared at him. 'What the hell does that mean?'

'You and Sarah were once ... romantically linked, yes?' he asked.

'Yes. We were a couple.' Ruth couldn't believe that in 2021, a senior police officer like Vernier found it difficult to discuss a gay relationship.

He raised his shoulders. 'Then you see each other after all this time ... and Sarah has had sex with many men ...'

'She was forced into being an escort!'

'So you say. Maybe you have a row last night. Or a disagreement.'

'No, we didn't. That's not what happened.'

'And maybe Sarah decided this morning that there is no future for you two,' he suggested. 'She calls a friend, an *uncle*, and he comes to pick her up from the hospital.'

Ruth took a few seconds. She was getting nowhere and Vernier wasn't interested in listening to her.

'No. That's not what happened,' Ruth muttered across the table. 'You need to be out there looking for her right now. Otherwise they will take her out of the country or they will kill her.'

'The best I can do is record her as a possible missing person,' he announced, 'and I need details from you so I can fill out one of these cards.'

'Are you kidding me?' Ruth seethed through gritted teeth.

There was a pause as she tried to gather her thoughts. Her trust in the Paris Police was limited and she had her suspicions that there was some form of corruption going on. There had been the failed operation at the offices of Global Escorts in Paris, and events at the farmhouse had clearly shown there had been a tip-off regarding the imminent police raid.

There was no way that she was going to divulge what Sarah had told her about the murder she had witnessed in 2013. She knew how powerful and rich a man like Patrice Le Bon was.

She wondered if his influence in the city stretched to its police force too.

She remembered what she had seen out of the window from the café.

'You were at the hospital at the time Sarah went missing, weren't you?' Ruth asked.

Vernier bristled. 'Yes. My officers have been talking to some of the women that we rescued yesterday.'

'But none of your officers saw anything?'

'No,' Vernier sighed. 'I'm not sure what you're trying to say.'

I'm getting nowhere. It's time to cut my losses and get out of here.

'I think we're done here,' she fumed as she stood up.

Vernier gave her a withering look. 'I am sure that I don't need to remind you that you are a British police officer and have no jurisdiction here.'

'I'm more than aware of that,' Ruth replied, but she knew it wasn't going to stop her. 'And you've made it very clear exactly how much help you're going to give me. So, I'm going to go and find Sarah myself.'

'In that case,' Vernier sneered as he raised an eyebrow, '... please be very careful. This city is extremely dangerous if you don't know your way around.'

Ruth went to the door. 'Don't worry. I'm from South London. I know how to handle myself thanks.'

She left his office and closed the door with enough force to register her annoyance.

CHAPTER 10

The DGSE headquarters (the Centre Administratif des Tourelles, codenamed CAT) was located at 141 boulevard Mortier in the 20th arrondissement to the east of Paris. Ruth had received a message from Stephen Flaherty in which he mentioned that he had worked with Agent Camille Moreau at the DGSE and found her to be professional and trustworthy. Ruth had managed to contact Moreau and arranged to see her straightaway. If Ruth couldn't persuade the Paris Police to help her look for Sarah, then maybe the French intelligence service might take her more seriously.

Having met at her first floor office, Moreau had suggested the more pleasant surroundings of the top floor café that looked across the Parisienne skyline.

Moreau returned from the servery and put Ruth's Americano coffee down on their table beside a huge plate glass window that had views over the city. 'Here you go.'

'Thank you,' Ruth replied, her mind still racing. She knew there was a ticking clock in her efforts to find Sarah. The longer Sarah was gone, the less likely it was that she would be found.

'I understand that you know Stephen Flaherty from the London Met's Missing Persons Unit?' Ruth asked, looking over at Moreau. Her hair was stylish, with dark lowlights. She had an interesting face which looked a little masculine but was still attractive. As with many native Parisians, she appeared effortlessly stylish and elegant.

'Yes. I have worked with Stephen on many cases over the years,' she confirmed.

Ruth took a sip of her coffee. It was bitter and strong but just what she needed. 'He says I can trust you.'

A smile tugged at Moreau's lips. 'That was nice of him to say. Especially in this city.'

'I need your help.'

'I understand that your friend Sarah discharged herself from hospital yesterday after we spoke in the café?'

Ruth raised an eyebrow. 'That's what the hospital told me.'

'You don't believe them?' Moreau asked dubiously.

'It's more complicated than that. And it's hard to know what I can and can't tell you.'

'My understanding is that Sarah had been working as an escort for Global Escorts for some time?'

'I think so. I know she had been in Paris for over two years.'

'She was an addict, no?'

'Yes. How did you know that?'

'Every sex worker in Paris is an addict. It's how the gangs control them. Even the €1,000-a-night escorts are addicts. It's why they find it so hard to leave. And maybe that is why your friend decided to discharge herself.'

'You think she left the hospital to score drugs?' Ruth asked.

'Don't you? You are an experienced detective. You know what terrible things people will do to get a fix. If she was scared and she needed to score, doesn't it make sense that she would leave?'

'She didn't leave on her own,' Ruth explained. 'A man claiming to be her uncle spoke to her and helped her to fill out the self-discharge papers. Then he wheeled her out of the hospital.'

'You think she was intimidated into going with this man?'

'Yes. She knew I was coming back to see her. You saw me getting her a drink from the café. It doesn't make any sense.'

'What do the police say?' Moreau asked.

Ruth grimaced. 'They're not interested. I was told that because there is no obvious crime, they won't use their resources to look for her.'

Moreau tutted. 'This doesn't surprise me.'

'I'm afraid that now they've got her back, they will kill her,' Ruth admitted.

Moreau frowned. 'Why? I think they will make her work for them again. Not in Paris, but somewhere in the world. Why do you think they will kill her? She is a valuable asset to them.'

Ruth hesitated. 'It's hard for me to know how much to tell you.'

Moreau looked directly at her. 'You can tell me as much as you would tell Stephen.'

'I tell Stephen everything.'

'Okay, then tell me.'

Fuck it. I need this woman's help and expertise. This is a risk worth taking.

'In 2013, at a sex party in London, Sarah witnessed the murder of a teenage girl by a high ranking British peer.'

'Mon Dieu,' she muttered under her breath.

'It's so shocking.'

Moreau's eyes widened. 'And no one knows about this?'

'No. She was the only witness,' Ruth explained as she shook her head. 'That's the problem. You know Sergei Saratov?'

Moreau shrugged. 'Of course.'

'Sarah witnessed both Sergei Saratov and Patrice Le Bon at the scene of the murder making a plan to get rid of the girl's body and to cover up what had happened.'

Moreau sat forward and asked, 'And Sarah heard all this?'

'Yes. That's how she was coerced into faking her own disappearance and eventually working for them as an escort. She was told that if she didn't, they would kill me and her.'

Moreau shook her head. 'That is shocking.'

Well that's got her bloody interest.

'Yes, it is. And that's why I think they might now decide to kill her to keep her quiet.'

'Then she is in great danger.'

'I know. That's why I need your help to find her.'

'Of course. I will do everything I can,' Moreau reassured her with a serious expression. 'You know we have been trying to build a case against Patrice Le Bon for many years?'

'Yes, and if Sarah was willing to testify, you could put Le Bon in prison.'

'Exactly.' Moreau paused, then frowned. 'Have you told the Paris Police any of this?' The tone of her question was one of concern.

'I spoke to Capitaine Vernier. I only told him that I thought Sarah might have been forced to leave the hospital and that I wanted his help to find her. I didn't tell him anything about the murder she'd witnessed.'

'My guess is that he was less than helpful?'

Ruth gave a half-hearted sneer. 'Yes. He said there was nothing he could do.'

'Please, do not tell the police anything more about what you have told me,' Moreau said forcibly. 'At best, they are incompetent and old fashioned. At worst, they are corrupt. Please, say no more to them.'

Ruth nodded in understanding. 'Of course.'

Taking a card from her pocket, Moreau scribbled a number on the back and handed it to her. 'Here. This is my personal cell phone number. Call me if there are any problems. What hotel are you staying at?'

'The Terrass Hotel in Montmartre.'

'I know it. Text me so that I have your cell phone number. And don't worry, I will do everything in my power to find Sarah and get her back.'

CHAPTER 11

It was early afternoon by the time Ruth got back to the hospital. She had managed to make phone calls to Ella and Nick to keep them updated. Stephen Flaherty hadn't answered his phone, but she had left a message and sent him an email to inform him about her conversations with both Vernier and Moreau.

Although this was personal, she knew that she needed to tap into all the experience she had of being a police officer. Essentially she was working on a missing person's case and so, despite her emotional attachment which was sending her head off in all sorts of directions, she needed to remain completely focussed and methodical. It was going to be easier said than done.

Her first port of call had to be the hospital security centre. She needed access to the CCTV from that morning to see the moment Sarah had left the hospital. Who was the man who had turned up claiming to be her uncle? Were there any obvious signs of coercion? She also needed CCTV for the car park to see what mode of transport had been used to take her. Had someone picked her up outside? Had they parked in the hospital car park?

She had been unable to make contact with Trelford yet. Without his help, or the aid of the Paris Police, she feared that she would not be able to make herself understood. Not only that, she had no jurisdiction in France and therefore probably wouldn't be entitled to access the hospital's CCTV. She knew from experience that even UK hospital security guards could be obstructive and demand the correct paperwork. They were generally 'jobsworth' pains in the arse!

Having made a botched attempt to make herself understood at the hospital reception, she spotted a man in a white short-sleeved shirt with an official-looking badge that read *Agent De Sécurité*. Even with her woeful command of the language, she could make an educated guess that he was a security guard – so she followed him.

She made her way down the central atrium on the ground floor, and remained a short distance behind as he turned left down a corridor. At the far end, he stopped by a door, tapped in a security code and went in.

Great. How is this going to work?

A few seconds later, Ruth arrived at the door and saw the security code pad on the wall beside it. Taking out her warrant card, she knocked on the door and prepared to try to bullshit her way inside.

The officer she had been following opened the door. He frowned when he saw her holding up her British Police identification.

'Hi there. Do you speak English?' she asked slowly.

He motioned with his hand. 'A little.'

'I am a police officer from the UK,' she explained, gesturing to her warrant card. 'I am looking for someone who left the hospital today.'

'Okay. You come in.' He stood back and ushered her into the security office. To the left, there was a bank of television screens linked to the CCTV cameras inside the hospital. Another officer sat back in a chair, eating a sandwich and gazing up at them apathetically.

Bingo!

'Yes, how can I help, Madame?' the officer asked. 'I do not understand.'

Ruth immediately pointed to the bank of screens. 'I need to see the CCTV from this morning. I am looking for someone. She is from the UK. I need to see when she left the hospital.'

The officer looked confused. 'You have spoken to the police here in Paris?'

'Yes. They know I'm here,' she lied.

He shook his head. 'I am sorry, Madame. Unless it is a French police officer, then I cannot let you see this. Maybe you ask the Paris Police and they can come with you?'

Bollocks! That's not going to happen any time soon.

Realising that this was a lost cause, Ruth gave him friendly smile. 'Yes.

I'll come back if that's okay.'

'I am sorry I cannot help you, Madame,' he said as he gestured to the door, 'but maybe you can come back?'

'Yes, thank you,' Ruth replied as she left and the door closed behind her. She would have a rethink.

Marching down the corridor, her next port of call was to go back to the ward on the third floor to clarify, as best she could, exactly what had happened when Sarah had discharged herself. There might be a clue in her behaviour or what she had said.

Ruth entered the lift and soon found herself back at the ward where she had briefly been that morning. She scoured the faces of the staff at the nurses' station but didn't recognise any of them. It wasn't surprising. She had been in such shock at

Sarah's sudden departure that she hadn't taken much notice of anything around her.

She went over to the group of nurses, who were talking in hushed tones. 'Excuse me please, does anyone here speak English?' she asked with a smile.

A young African nurse nodded. 'Yes.'

'I'm a British police officer,' Ruth said as she held out her ID card. 'You had a British patient in here this morning. Her name was Sophie Collins?'

'Yes, I remember her.'

'Were you here this morning?'

'Yes, I'm about to finish my shift now but I was here this morning. You came just after she left?'

'Yes, I did,' Ruth replied.

'You seemed upset.'

Ruth didn't want to give too much away. 'I was confused. I didn't understand why Sophie had discharged herself.'

The nurse shrugged. 'It happens all the time with ...' She took a few moments to think of the right words to describe 'Sophie'. 'How do you say, toxicomane?'

Ruth looked perplexed. 'Sorry, I don't understand.'

The nurse then turned and spoke in French to the other nurses before continuing. 'Addict? You say drug addict?'

Although it was hard to hear Sarah described as a drug addict, Ruth nodded. 'Yes. Drug addict.'

'Yes. They come in here for a day or two. They have been beaten. Then they sign the forms and they go.'

'She was a friend of mine. Do you know where she was going or why she left?'

'I think she was going with her uncle.'

'Yes. Could you tell me what he looked like?'

'A tall man. Maybe he was 40 years old. And a very pale face.'

'Anything else?'

'He was wearing a baseball cap and glasses.'

'Was he French?'

'No,' she replied, 'he had some kind of accent. I think Polish or Russian maybe? I know he wasn't her uncle of course.'

'How do you mean?' Ruth asked.

The nurse pulled a face. 'You know. He was her souteneur. Le marlou. How you say ... her pimp, yes?'

'Yes, maybe.' Ruth smiled politely. It was another difficult thing to hear about Sarah.

She was starting to feel a little overwhelmed.

CHAPTER 12

'I feel like I should be there with you, Mum,' Ella said.

'It really wouldn't be a good idea, darling,' Ruth assured her as she shifted the pillows on her hotel bed. 'I've got to spend tomorrow looking for her and God knows what kinds of places I'm going to find myself in.'

'I'll stay at the hotel then,' Ella suggested. 'At least you would have someone to talk to when you got back.'

'I'm talking to you now, silly. And I'll need all your help and support when I get home. But I need to focus on finding Sarah while I'm here. Okay?'

'Okay,' Ella replied. 'I just worry about you.'

'I know you do. And just talking to you like this really helps. So, I'm going to run myself a hot bath, order room service, and watch a movie.'

'Ring me tomorrow as soon as you find out anything. Promise?'

'Of course,' Ruth replied. 'Night darling.'

'Night Mum.'

Ruth put her mobile phone down. She had returned to the Terrass Hotel an hour ago feeling utterly exhausted. She needed time to sit, think, and plan her next move. Sarah had been somehow coerced into leaving. Having lived in fear for the past seven years, it wouldn't have been difficult to intimidate and pressure her into discharging herself. If she was an addict, then the offer of heroin might also have done the trick. Either way, Ruth was convinced that Sarah was back in the hands of the men who had controlled and sold her through Global Escorts.

Ruth's phone rang. It was Stephen.

'Ruth? I got your last message. Have you heard anything since then?'

'No, I'm going to start to look for her again first thing tomorrow.'

'Okay. I have two Scotland Yard detectives who have been investigating what they believe is a high-level sex trafficking ring involving politicians and other VIPs. They're very keen to fly out and do what they can to find Sarah. I don't think they'll get there until the day after tomorrow though.'

'That's fine,' Ruth replied. It would be good to have experienced UK police officers to help. 'Your friend Camille Moreau at the DGSE has told me to give the Paris Police a wide berth.'

'Not the first time I've heard that,' Stephen admitted.

'It does however limit my access to certain places.'

'Oliver Trelford might be able to help you with that,' he suggested. 'My advice would be to keep what you learn close to your chest as much as you can.'

'Anything else your end?' she asked.

'I think we have a possible identity for the girl that Sarah believes she saw murdered in November 2013,' Stephen stated. 'Gabriella Cardoso. She was seventeen at the time. She had come to London to work as an au pair for a family in Holland Park. The father was some kind of city hedge funder. She told the family that she was going out with friends in Notting Hill on Friday November 1st 2013, and never came home. There was a police investigation but there was a suggestion that she might have travelled to Australia to meet up with backpacker friends from Portugal out there. There is no record of her travelling out of the country in the days after her disappearance.'

'Do you have a photograph?' Ruth asked.

'Yes. There's one in her file. She was a very pretty girl and had been asked to do some modelling while she was in London. The mother of the family remembers thinking that Gabriella was wearing a dress that night and looked very glamorous. She thought it was strange as she was only meant to be going to a pub in Notting Hill.'

'Do we know if there was a Secret Garden party that night?' Ruth asked, thinking out loud.

'I can't find anything at the moment. Obviously they don't make a habit of keeping accessible records.'

'That timeframe fits in, doesn't it?'

'Seven people went missing over that week in London, but Gabriella is the only one that fits the profile. I'll send a photo over for you. When you find Sarah, you can see if she can identify her.'

'When? You seem very confident!'

'Bloody hell, Ruth. You've been looking for her for seven years,' Stephen said in a voice hard with resolve. 'There is no way you're going to let her go now you're this close, is there?'

'No, there isn't.' Ruth felt encouraged by his words.

'I'll call again tomorrow,' he promised. 'And good luck, Ruth.'

'Thank you for everything, Stephen,' she said as she ended the call.

With a deep sigh she nestled back into the pillows and tried to take stock of where she was with everything.

There was a knock at the door.

Ruth sat up and felt uneasy.

Who's that? I'm not expecting anyone, am I?

Wrapping her hotel gown around her and fastening the cord, she walked over to the door.

'Hello?' she asked.

There was no reply.

The person on the other side of the door knocked again.

Either they hadn't heard her or they didn't want to respond.

'Hello, who is it?' Ruth asked, now feeling anxious.

'Hi Ruth,' said a voice she immediately recognised.

What the fuck!

She opened the door and saw that Nick was standing there with a wry smile.

'Or should I say *Bonjour*?' he asked.

'What the hell are you doing here?' she asked, her eyes wide with disbelief.

Nick laughed. 'Oh that's bloody charming, that is!'

Ushering him into the room, she shook her head in bewilderment. 'I don't think I've ever been so glad to see you!'

They hugged for a few seconds.

Nick grinned. 'I've got the room at the end of the corridor, if that's all right?'

Twenty minutes later, Ruth and Nick were sitting at the hotel's chic rooftop bar with stunning views over the city.

Ruth took her glass of wine and raised it. 'Well cheers. I'm glad you're here, even if it's for horrible reasons.'

'Salut,' Nick said, lifting his Diet Coke. He was several years sober and Ruth found his ongoing sobriety and adherence to AA's 12-step programme incredibly impressive.

'That's Spanish, you plank!'

'Is it?' he asked with a grin. 'What's French for cheers then?'

'I don't know actually,' Ruth admitted. 'I can't believe you came out here.'

There was a gleam in his eye as he spoke. 'I didn't have much choice actually.'

'How do you mean?'

'Have you met my fiancée?' he joked.

Ruth had known Amanda for years and was godmother to their daughter Megan. She also knew that Amanda was very headstrong and not to be messed with.

Ruth laughed. 'Yeah, and I wouldn't cross her!'

'Exactly,' Nick said and then sipped his drink. 'She told me that you needed my help, to pack my bags, and get my arse out here. So, ta-da, here I am.'

'What did Drake say?' Ruth asked. DCI Drake was head of Llancastell CID and their line manager.

Nick shrugged. 'He said I was owed some holiday and there was nothing pressing that needed my immediate attention.'

Ruth smiled. 'You do know that now we're here we'll have some terrible outbreak of serious crime in North Wales.'

'Naturally,' Nick chortled, and then pointed out at the skyline. 'So, where is the Stade de France?'

'The what?'

'Where France play rugby. Wales are playing them there in a few weeks' time. October.'

'You and bloody rugby.' Ruth rolled her eyes. Then she stared at him. The lines of tiny lights that were strung across the rooftop bar flickered on his face. 'God, it's really good to see you.'

Nick returned her stare with a serious expression. 'I can't believe everything that's happened in the past few days. And I can't believe you saw and spoke to Sarah and now she's gone again!'

'I'm going to find her.'

'No. *We're* going to find her,' Nick reassured her. 'What have we got?'

'I'm not sure where to start ... She's incredibly scared because of what she witnessed seven years ago and everything she's been through since then. She has no passport, phone or money. She's a heroin addict, which is likely to mean she will be looking to score. The man who helped her leave the hospital told the nurses he was her uncle. They assumed he was her pimp.'

'Any idea who he was?'

'No. Tall, thin, 40s, possibly a Russian accent. He was wearing a baseball cap and glasses.'

'Russian accent?'

'I know. We know that Sergei Saratov is behind Global Escorts, so that might fit with that,' Ruth said thinking out loud. 'I think this man, whoever he was, scared Sarah into discharging herself. And I assume there were others waiting somewhere outside the hospital to whisk her away somewhere.'

'CCTV?" Nick asked.

'Yeah, that's the problem. I have no jurisdiction here. I asked to see the hospital CCTV and drew a blank.'

'Can't you get a warrant from the Paris Police?'

'Firstly, they're not interested. Secondly, I've been told to keep my distance from them. Inept at best, totally corrupt at worst - I think that was the summary.'

'Christ!' Nick pulled a face. 'What about this Patrice Le Bon fella?'

Ruth raised her eyebrow. 'You have been doing your homework, haven't you?'

'Of course.'

'He owns some model agencies and he is very rich and well connected. He also has political ambitions. Lots of friends in very high places,' she informed him. 'Strong suspicions that Saratov used him to recruit high-class sex workers and help run their global sex trafficking ring.'

'You think Le Bon is paying off Paris coppers?'

'I wouldn't be surprised. A few weeks ago, there was a police operation against the Global Escorts offices and premises in Paris. By the time they got there, everyone had cleared out. The only mistake they made was leaving some of the girls' passports behind.'

Nick rubbed his hand through his beard. 'They were tipped off?'

'How else did they know the raid was going to go ahead? They shipped everyone out to a place south of Paris, a farmhouse in the Forêt de Sénart. Paris Police set up surveillance, but by the time we raided it two days ago the place had started to be cleared out. And they rigged the computers with explosives which they triggered when we arrived. It destroyed any evidence on the premises. The Paris Police were left with some Eastern European thugs and about a dozen trafficked sex workers, one of which was Sarah.'

'Okay. We need to find this mystery man who was at the hospital this morning.'

Ruth drained her glass and looked over at him. 'Early night and start again at dawn?'

'Sounds good to me,' he replied, getting up from the table.

'And Nick?'

'Yeah?'

'Thank you for coming out here,' she said with a serious expression.

Nick shrugged. 'Running around Paris with you, or paperwork in North Wales? It was a no-brainer!'

CHAPTER 13

The sun was just starting to rise as Ruth and Nick drove his hire car through Paris, heading south west towards the Hôpital Européen Georges-Pompidou. A warm haze of burnt orange shrouded the eastern horizon of the city behind them. The traffic was thankfully still light as they made good progress past the Arc de Triomphe, and then west towards the boulevards des Maréchaux, the collection of thoroughfares that encircle the city. This led them all the way down through the city to a bridge over the Seine called the Pont du Gangliano. To their left, the dark shape of the Eiffel Tower seemed to have a strange blue hue in the early morning light.

'Have you been here before?' Ruth asked after ten minutes of comfortable silence. They had spent countless early mornings in cars together and seemed to be intuitive as to when and when not to speak.

'To Paris?' Nick asked.

'Yes, where else?'

'Ages ago. A few of us jumped in a car and got the ferry over. We watched France play Wales. Eighty thousand Frenchmen going mad and a tiny bunch of Welsh fans.'

'Did you win?'

'You know what? I drank so much that day,' Nick admitted, 'that when I woke the next morning I couldn't remember the score. But no, we didn't win. My mates all took the piss because I insisted that we had to go and see Jim Morrison's grave before we left Paris. As you know, I am a massive *Doors'* fan.'

'Yes I know, but you didn't tell me Jim Morrison is buried in Paris. I assumed he was buried in America.'

'No. His grave is in the Père Lachaise cemetery. I think that's how you pronounce it. There are lots of famous people buried there, like Oscar Wilde. Jim Morrison's grave is always covered with flowers from fans visiting and it's got this meaningful inscription in Greek. Something about a divine spirit.'

'Well, you learn something every day Nicholas.'

A few minutes later, they crossed over the Seine and the huge modern, glass structure of the hospital dominated the skyline.

'That's a hospital?' Nick asked as they followed the signs to the car park. 'It looks like an enormous art gallery.'

'I know. I guess that's the French for you. Stylish in everything they do,' Ruth said as he parked the car.

'Bit different to Llancastell University Hospital,' he quipped.

Ruth thought of the old, red brick buildings of the Victorian hospital in her home town and rolled her eyes. Then she spotted Oliver Trelford sitting on a bench close to the main entrance. She had arranged to meet him there.

'Trelford's here.'

'What's he like?' Nick asked, turning off the ignition.

'You'll hate him,' Ruth joked as they got out of the car.

'Why?'

'He has a posh English accent. Oxbridge.'

Nick arched his brows. 'Say no more.'

'He grows on you,' she said as they approached and Trelford stood up and gave them an awkward wave.

'What, like fungus?' Nick quipped under his breath.

Ruth smiled and indicated Nick. 'Oliver, this is DS Nick Evans. He's here to help me for a few days. Nick, this is Oliver Trelford from Interpol.'

They shook hands.

'What have we got, Oliver?' she asked.

'Very little my end, I'm afraid,' he replied. 'I'm getting nothing from any of my sources.'

'She can't get very far, can she?' Ruth said.

'No, I don't suppose she can. She didn't have any kind of cell phone that we could try to trace, did she?'

Ruth shook her head. 'Not that I'm aware of.'

'What we really need is the CCTV from the hospital,' Nick chimed in.

Ruth looked at Trelford. 'I'd like to get a look at the man who visited her claiming to be her uncle, but the security guards in there won't deal with British police.'

'It's beyond my jurisdiction. I'm afraid I'm in the same boat as you. We're probably relying on the Paris Police to help us with that.' Trelford said, raising a doubting brow.

'Well I won't hold my breath then,' Ruth sighed.

Trelford shrugged. 'Don't worry. We will find her.'

'Yes we will. I haven't come this far to lose her again.'

Trelford looked directly at her. 'And Ruth?'

'Yes?'

'The people who held her captive are very dangerous,' he warned. 'Be careful please. Both of you.'

Ruth and Nick approached the main entrance of the hospital. There were a few doctors and nurses arriving for shifts but otherwise the building seemed very quiet.

The sliding electronic doors parted and they went inside.

Ruth pointed over to the corridor where she had found the hospital's security office the day before. 'This way.'

'Erm, not to throw a spanner in the works this morning, but do you have a plan?' Nick asked.

'Not really ... Break in?'

'You want to break into the security office?'

'Don't worry,' she reassured him, 'something will come to me.'

They walked down the corridor and stopped outside the security office door.

'Got your warrant card?' she asked Nick.

Reaching into his jacket pocket, he pulled it out. 'Of course.'

She banged on the door and took out her own warrant card.

A few seconds later, an officer opened the door and looked at them both dubiously. He was in his 60s, overweight, and appeared very tired.

'Oui?' he asked.

They showed their warrant cards and he beckoned them in, mumbling something under his breath.

'Do you speak English?' Ruth asked as the door closed behind them.

He shrugged. 'Some.'

Looking around, she saw a younger-looking officer sitting by the bank of CCTV monitors. He had his feet up on the desk and earphones in his ears.

Nick put his hand on Ruth's shoulder. 'Don't worry, I've got this.'

She watched as he went over and nodded to the young man, who removed his earphones. 'Morning,' said Nick, with a cheery smile. 'We are police officers from the UK. Do you speak English?'

He took his feet off the desk. 'Yes, I speak some English.'

'Okay, great.' Nick smiled as he reached into his pocket. 'You a PSG fan?' He was talking about the main football team in Paris.

'No, no.'

'Paris FC then?' Nick asked. 'League two.'

This raised a smile. 'Of course. PSG are just some Arabic team. They are not French.' He was referring to the fact that PSG, or Paris St Germain, had been owned by the Arabic country Qatar since 2011.

'Yeah, I agree.' Nick removed his hand from his pocket. He was holding some euros and a computer memory stick. 'I have a little proposition for you. You know what un cadeau is?'

'Yes, of course.'

Even with her limited French knowledge, Ruth was pretty sure that cadeau meant present.

'Okay, great,' Nick said with a grin. 'Now we need to see the hospital CCTV from yesterday morning. Let's say 6am to midday. We also need to see the footage from the car park.'

'Okay.'

Nick gestured to the computers that were banked up to the left-hand side of the monitors. 'I'm guessing you've got all that footage on MPEG or MP4 files?'

'MP4, yes,' the young man replied, nodding.

'Brilliant!' Nick laughed. Ruth gave him a look as if to say *What the bloody hell are you doing?* but they hadn't been thrown out yet so she would see what happened next.

Nick waved the memory stick. 'Okay, so I'm going to give you this, and you're going to copy the files onto it. In return for that ...' Nick held out four €50 notes, 'I'm going to give you un cadeau. How does that sound?'

The young man looked interested.

Please god let this crude attempt at bribery work! Ruth thought to herself.

'Okay,' he said, holding out his hand.

Nick gave him the money and the memory stick.

'We have a deal?' he asked, just to clarify.

'Oui, mon ami. We have a deal.'

Back in the hotel room, Nick opened his laptop and inserted the memory stick. Ruth looked at him and shook her head. 'I still have no idea how you thought that would work,' she said with a wry smile.

Nick smiled back. 'I read recently that Paris is the most corrupt city in Europe. They've just charged their ex-President Sarkozy with years of bribery and corruption. I just think it's a cultural thing.'

'I don't care what it is,' Ruth laughed. 'It bloody worked.'

Nick began to search the files for what they were looking for. After a few failed attempts, he found footage from the camera that covered the hospital's main entrance.

'Okay. We're looking for a man, 40, tall, baseball cap and glasses. He has to have arrived at the hospital any time in the morning and left around 11am.'

Nick began to whizz through the footage, slowing it down every time there was anyone who might vaguely fit the description.

After fifteen minutes of scrolling backwards and forwards, he cast his eyes to Ruth. 'Sorry. There's no one matching that description.'

'But we know that Sarah discharged herself somewhere near 11am, so when they leave they must appear on this footage?'

Checking the timecode, Nick played the footage forward slowly.

Where is the man who came to speak to her and where is Sarah?

The timecode hit midday and Nick looked doubtful. 'Where the bloody hell are they?'

Ruth sighed. Time was ticking on and they were getting nowhere. 'What are we missing here? I assume they must have left the hospital together.'

'Which means they didn't leave via the main entrance,' Nick deduced, thinking out loud.

Taking her phone, Ruth searched the Internet quickly.

'Shit! There's an employees' entrance on the south side of the building,' she exclaimed.

Nick scanned the files on the memory stick. 'Bingo! L'entrée des employés?'

'Sounds about right,' Ruth beamed.

Pulling up the image from the camera over the employees' entrance, Nick repeated the process from before. They watched the timecode carefully, and at 10.23am a tall man in a baseball cap used a security code to gain access through the employees' entrance.

'That must be him!' Ruth exclaimed.

Nick froze the footage. 'I can't do much with the image on this laptop I'm afraid.'

'Can you make it any bigger?'

'I'll give it a go,' he said as he zoomed in.

The man's face now filled the screen. There was something about him that struck a chord with Ruth. She had seen him somewhere before.

'What colour is his hair?' she asked.

Nick leaned forward and squinted for a better look. 'I think it's white.'

'Yes, that's what I thought.' Ruth searched her memory for where she had seen the man before. 'Oh my God, I saw him outside the hospital about half an hour after this.'

'Are you sure?'

'Positive. I remember wondering if he was some kind of albino. He was standing outside with that Capitaine Vernier.'

Nick's eyes widened. 'What? Isn't this the man we think threatened Sarah and probably took her from the hospital?'

'Yes.' Ruth could hardly believe it herself. 'But I've seen him somewhere before.'

Then it came to her. She strode across the hotel room, grabbed her briefcase, and pulled out the folders of things that she had collected over the years. She shuffled through some newspaper clippings. One of the articles from *The Times* centred on allegations that had been made against Patrice Le Bon. There was a photograph of Le Bon with several other men.

On the far left was the man with white hair.

Somehow she had registered his face or his appearance as being out of the ordinary and it had stuck in her memory.

'Here,' she said as she pointed to the photo in the paper. 'Is this him?'

Nick peered at it for a few seconds and then nodded. 'Yeah. The long white hair and the nose. I'm pretty sure it's him.'

'Right.' Ruth's thoughts were racing around her head. 'So, this is the man who came and spoke to Sarah in the ward and took her out of the hospital.'

Nick continued to play the footage forward. They still needed to check when the man and Sarah left the hospital. As the timecode showed 10.52 am, two figures came past the camera, now walking out of the hospital via the employees' entrance. Even though they weren't facing the camera, it was clear that it was the white-haired man and Sarah. She was no longer in a wheelchair.

Nick paused the image. 'This is why we didn't see either of them leaving via the main entrance.'

Examining the screen closely, Ruth spotted something. 'Can you make that bigger for me?'

Nick obliged.

Ruth looked again. The man's right hand was gripped around the back of Sarah's left arm – he was forcibly leading her from the hospital.

'Doesn't look like she left of her own accord,' Nick observed.

'No,' Ruth agreed. 'It looks like he is frog-marching her out. Can we check the car park CCTV now?'

Switching the screen back to all of the files, Nick spotted the one labelled *Parking* and soon found a high CCTV camera that gave a bird's eye view of the whole car park. He moved it forward to 10.52 am.

'What if employees park somewhere else?' Ruth asked.

Suddenly, the man and Sarah appeared on the screen walking towards a 4x4 car that was waiting in a parking bay. The back door opened and the man shoved Sarah inside. He didn't get into the car with her, but instead closed the door and the 4x4 sped away.

Ruth took a moment to think. 'Jesus! This man shoved Sarah into the car. He then walked around to the other side of the car park where he spoke to Vernier. They both got in a BMW 4x4 and drove off.'

Nick shook his head. 'So we know Vernier is bent.'

'And probably being paid off by Le Bon.'

Nick rewound the footage so that they had a clear view of the car that had taken Sarah. He zoomed in on its licence plate.

'Lexus SUV, plate EK-366-AS,' he said, reading from the screen as Ruth scribbled it down.

Nick sat back on the chair and gave her a satisfied look. 'Not bad for a morning's work. How do we find out who this man is and who that car belongs to?'

Ruth grabbed her phone and tapped in a number. 'I know exactly who can help with this.'

The phone rang and then a voice answered, 'Camille Moreau.'

'Camille, it's Ruth Hunter.'

'Ruth. I was hoping to speak to you this morning,' Moreau said. 'I have a couple of developments I wanted to share with you.'

'So do I,' Ruth said. 'If I send you a photo of someone, could you tell me if you recognise him?'

'Of course. You want to do that right now?'

'Yes, if you can hold on? I'll take a photo and then text it to you.' Ruth laid out the newspaper article which showed the picture of Patrice Le Bon with a group of men. She focussed her camera on the white-haired man's angular face, took a photo, and texted it to Moreau.

'Okay, I've got it,' Moreau said. 'I'm just having a look now.'

'Great.'

'Yes, I know who this man is,' she said in a very serious tone. 'His name is Milan Golkin. I think you should come to my office right away.'

CHAPTER 14

Ruth and Nick were sitting in Moreau's neat office in the DGSE building. The slatted blinds had been closed and the only light was from her desk lamp. She handed a thick file over to Ruth, who couldn't help but notice Moreau's slender hands, immaculate French-tipped nails, and the lack of a wedding ring on her left hand.

I wonder if she's gay, she thought in that fleeting moment.

'This is everything we have on Milan Golkin,' Moreau explained. 'He was a Colonel in the Spetsnaz.'

'What's that?' Nick asked.

'Russian special forces. They are controlled by the main military intelligence service, the GRU.'

Ruth looked confused. 'Maybe I've watched too many films but I thought the KGB was the Russian intelligence agency?'

Moreau shook her head. 'The KGB was effectively a state-run, secret police force and has had little power in recent years. The GRU has no time for the KGB. It thinks it's old fashioned and obsolete. The GRU is military intelligence and sees itself as far superior. At the turn of the millennium, Golkin virtually ran an elite unit called 29155.'

'Catchy,' Nick joked.

'What did they do?' Ruth asked.

'Foreign assassinations, covert operations. You remember the poisonings in Salisbury in 2018?'

Ruth nodded. 'Of course.'

How could she forget the poisoning of Sergei Skripal and his daughter in the seemingly leafy and harmless Wiltshire city of Salisbury in March that year. Skripal was a former Russian military officer and a double agent for the British Secret Intelligence Service. The British government eventually accused Russia of attempted murder, and retaliated by expelling many Russian diplomats.

'Alexander Petrov and Ruslan Boshirov, the two men suspected of the poisoning, are GRU Unit 29155 agents.'

Ruth looked slightly shocked. 'And Golkin still runs this special unit?'

Moreau shook her head. 'No. Five years ago he went rogue.'

'Meaning?' Nick asked.

'I suppose it means freelance. He sold his services to the highest bidder.'

'Patrice Le Bon?' Ruth guessed.

'Correct. Le Bon has been one of his employers, along with Sergei Saratov.'

Ruth let out an exaggerated sigh. 'Which is why he was at the hospital and why we saw him taking Sarah from there and into a waiting car.'

'How do we find Golkin?' Nick asked.

'My honest answer is that you don't.'

'Why not? We're experienced police officers.'

'Golkin is a psychopath. He's incredibly dangerous.'

After a brief silence, Ruth got up out of her chair. 'I'm sorry, Camille. We're not going back to the UK without Sarah.'

'You two need to listen to what I have to say to you. You are now out of your depth,' Moreau warned. 'If you go after Golkin you'll probably end up seriously injured or dead.'

Nick got up, casting his eyes from Ruth to Moreau. 'Well, we'll just have to take our chances then, won't we?

Nick and Ruth pulled up outside a beautiful 19th century apartment block on rue Garreau in Montmartre. It was where Global Escorts had been based before the police raid a few weeks ago. Ruth had used the journey to ring Trelford and update him on what they had found. Even he seemed shocked that she had seen Vernier and Golkin talking together outside the hospital. He promised to talk to his various contacts and get back to her as soon as possible.

Rue Garreau was narrow, and a parking space had been set aside for around twenty scooters that were parked in a long line. Beside that was an old zebra crossing, its white lines faded and in need of new paint.

'Is this the place?' Nick asked as they got out of the car.

'Yes, it's the address I got from Stephen Flaherty.'

It was getting hot, and the cream painted façade seemed to glow in the sun's rays. The double doors that led into the building from the pavement were painted a subtle shade of blue, and were criss-crossed by yellow police tape that read *Entrée Interdite*. Glancing up, Ruth thought that the building couldn't look more French if it tried. Each floor had a small balcony with ornate iron railings, and pots filled with brightly coloured flowers. In the middle of each balcony was a double glass and wooden door, and on each side of it were windows with white shutters.

As she glanced around, she spotted an old-fashioned Parisienne bar called *Bar Chez Gus* on the opposite corner. It was a place that Sarah had mentioned in the hospital. A couple of elderly men sat at tables outside, smoking, drinking and soaking up the sun on their leathery faces. Ruth could smell the tobacco from their filterless cigarettes and immediately wanted one herself. She would have to wait until they'd had a look around.

'We need to go in here first,' she said, pointing to the bar.

'Bit early for a beer, isn't it?' Nick joked.

Ruth gave him a sarcastic smile as they crossed the street.

Even though it was sunny outside, the inside of the bar was a little dark and dingy. It was virtually empty. There were simple wooden chairs and tables with wine glasses and cutlery set out on them. A blackboard on the wall to the side of the bar carried the day's menu scrawled in chalk.

Ruth walked over to the young barman who was polishing glasses. 'Good morning. Do you speak English?'

He shrugged unhelpfully.

'I'm looking for Gus,' she said.

'Gus? Yes.' He put his cloth and glass on the counter and walked into a room at the back.

A moment later, a man in his late 60s, moustache, cardigan and thick glasses, came round the bar. Ruth assumed this was Gus.

'Yes, can I help you?' he asked.

Ruth pulled out her warrant card. Even in Paris, it got people's attention and prevented anyone thinking she was just some crazy tourist. 'We're British police officers. We're looking for Gus, the man who owns this bar.'

'Okay. Am I in some kind of trouble?'

Nick smiled and shook his head. 'No, no.'

Taking out her mobile phone, Ruth got a photo of Sarah up on the screen and showed it to him.

'I'm looking for this woman,' she said.

Gus peered carefully at the phone and then shook his head. 'No, sorry. I do not know her.'

Ruth lowered her voice and gestured to the apartment block across the road. 'Her real name is Sarah but you will probably know her as Amandine. She was one of the women who worked across there.'

'I don't know her. Sorry,' he said dismissively as he made his way over to the bar and began to tidy away some glasses.

Ruth approached him again and he glared at her.

'I told you that I do not know her,' he muttered. 'Now please, leave.'

He's definitely rattled, Ruth thought.

'She told me about you, Gus. I was at the hospital with her yesterday and she told me about this place and about you.'

He continued to ignore her and carried on clearing away glasses and plates.

'She said you were a very kind man. That you helped her and her friends. She's a very good friend of mine. Please, Gus,' she pleaded, 'I need your help to find her.'

He turned to look at her, then put the dirty glasses down on the bar. 'She is your friend?' he asked in a virtual whisper.

'Yes.'

'Really?'

'She told me how you gave her a glass of ice, a coke, and salt and vinegar crisps every time she came in here.'

His eyes widened.

Ruth gave an audible sigh. 'Can you help me find her? Please.'

He nodded very slowly. 'Yes. I do know her. She did tell me her name was Amandine, but I knew she was lying. She is English.'

'Yes, she's English.' Ruth was relieved she was making some kind of progress. 'Has she been here recently?'

He shook his head. 'Not since the police came to the apartments. I'm sorry. I was very fond of her. We talked a lot. You say Sarah is her real name?'

'Yes, it is.'

He stroked the stubble on his chin. 'Sarah. Yes, that makes sense. She looks like a Sarah.'

'You knew her well?'

'Yes,' he replied, but she could sense that he was holding something back from her.

'And all the girls from over there came in here?' Nick asked.

He replied with a solemn nod.

Ruth fixed him with a look. 'What is it that you're not telling us?'

After a slight hesitation, Gus relented. 'There was man who lived above here. He sold them drugs. I don't like drugs but it is not my place to tell people what to do with their lives. So, the girls would go upstairs, get their drugs and maybe take them there. Then come down here and drink.'

'Did you know what was going on across the road?' Ruth asked, pointing to what had been the Global Escorts building.

'Of course. I am not stupid. There was nothing I could do. But I made sure they got food and I listened to them talk about their families and their homes,' he said with a mournful expression. 'It made me and my wife very sad to see them like that.'

Ruth took out a card that had her mobile phone number on it and handed it to him. 'If Sarah comes in here, or you see her, could you please call me on that number?'

'Of course. I will ask if anyone has seen her.'

'Thank you.'

They crossed back over the street and stood outside the former premises of Global Escorts.

'How do we get in?' Nick asked.

Ruth scanned her eyes over the doors and the first floor to look for a way in. There were thick wooden panels on the double doors at ground level. From there, the two shuttered balconies weren't that far above.

She turned to Nick and winked. 'Fancy giving me a boost?' Her body hadn't fully recovered from the explosion at the farmhouse yet, and the bruise at the centre of her back was still painful. She didn't care.

Nick looked up at the first floor balcony. 'Really? I just ...'

'If you make a joke about my age or weight I will kick you,' she warned. 'Come on.'

He platted the fingers of his hands together. 'Ready.'

She stepped onto his hands, and felt herself being raised up. At the same time, she pushed her right leg onto the ledge of a wooden panel on the door and stretched up.

Oh God, if this doesn't work I'm going to fall flat on my back.

Reaching up as high as she could, she felt a searing pain in her back. She grabbed hold of the stone ledge on the balcony, first with her left hand and then her right.

Don't look down whatever you do, she told herself.

She pushed down onto the top of the ground floor doors and simultaneously pulled herself up, grabbing hold of the top of the wrought iron railings. She swung her leg over and stood upright.

Bloody hell, that was unpleasant.

Now standing on the first floor balcony, she looked down at Nick. 'Still got it.'

'Impressive,' he called up. 'What if those balcony doors are locked?'

Ruth turned to the flimsy, long glass and wooden doors. She gave them an almighty kick and they flew open.

She shrugged down at Nick with a smile. 'Looks like they're open then.'

Stepping through the doors, she entered a bedroom. There was a huge bed with black satin sheets, a leather headboard, and an array of ties and handcuffs. The ceiling above was mirrored.

As she went over to the door, she noticed the lingering smell of perfume and body oil. It was a world away from some of the cheap brothels she had been to in South London and North Wales. However, the thought of Sarah in there with paying customers was distressing.

She walked down some carpeted stairs and came to the double doors that led to the street where Nick was standing. She slid back a series of bolts and locks and pulled the doors open.

As Nick came in, she realised that they were standing in some kind of reception area. It could have been for a boutique hotel or even a spa.

Nick looked around at the chic decor. 'First time I've been in a brothel like this.'

'That's elite escorts for you. The only things the police found of any note when they raided here were the passports of the twelve women and girls that were being held. Apparently, Sarah had a false passport under the name Amandine Thiney. I just want us to look around and see if they missed anything.'

Nick nodded. 'I'll go upstairs shall I?'

'Yeah.' Ruth went over to the large reception desk and sat down on the chair. As Nick disappeared upstairs, she rooted around in some old boxes of stationery. She then came across a Global Escorts brochure that advertised the women. It sickened her to see them laid out like objects to be rented in some catalogue.

Moving through the ground floor, it was clear that whoever had cleared the offices and the building, had done a good job. There was a kitchen area with an empty fridge. Beyond that, there was a bathroom.

As she surveyed the basic-looking bathroom, she looked over at the tiny frosted window. On a shelf nearby was a small potted plant. She picked it up instinctively, and noticed a tiny fragment of paper underneath. It had clearly been hidden. On it was written the name *Celestine* and a cell phone number, 03 27 43 97 98.

'Found something?' asked a voice. It was Nick.

She turned and showed him the piece of paper. 'This was hidden under a pot.'

'Celestine?' Nick took out his phone and dialled the number.

'Anything?' Ruth asked after a few seconds.

He shook his head. 'Nope. It's just ringing. Let's try it again later.'

'Find anything upstairs?' Ruth asked as they continued to move through the ground floor.

'Clean as a whistle,' he said. 'Someone did a very good job of cleaning this place and not leaving any evidence.'

Ruth parted some heavy burgundy curtains, and saw a pair of French windows that led out into a fairly grotty-looking outside space.

She opened them, and took a step into the small overgrown garden. Two old mattresses that were stained with blood rested ominously against the garden wall. The whole area smelled of old rubbish and urine.

This is nice, she thought ironically.

Suddenly there was a bang and the sound of male voices talking.

Nick looked at her.

Craning her neck to look back into the building, she saw two men with shaved heads and black jackets standing inside.

'Shit!' she whispered.

'Friend or foe?' Nick asked quietly.

'I don't know, but let's not hang around to find out.'

Nick pointed to the fence-topped wall at the bottom of the garden. It had to be ten feet high.

'Seriously?' Ruth grumbled.

This is bloody ridiculous.

Sprinting to the wall, Nick climbed onto its top and grabbed the mesh fence with his hands.

'Come on!' he panted urgently.

How the hell am I going to do this?

Glancing left, she could see that Nick already had one leg over the top of the fence.

Ruth got her footing and pushed herself up with all her strength.

She could hear the voices getting closer. Someone was coming towards the open doors. The voices were now shouting and becoming agitated.

Shit!

Nick reached down, grabbed her hand and pulled her up the fence.

'Here you go,' he gasped as he took her weight.

She scrambled up, rolled over the top of the fence and dropped down on the other side to join him.

'Thanks,' she panted.

'Any time.'

They were in a dark cobbled alleyway to the rear of the street.

Ruth glanced through the mesh in the fence.

The two men were now in the garden. A second later, one of them looked in their direction, pointed, and shouted something in French.

'Shit! They've seen us,' Ruth gasped.

'Run!' Nick shouted as they turned left and sprinted down the alleyway.

They ran full pelt and out into a side street.

Ruth was seriously out of breath and getting a stitch.

Bloody hell! I'm unfit.

Looking back, she could see that there was no sign of the men – yet.

They continued to jog, reaching a main road and finding themselves back on a busy one-way system.

Ruth looked at Nick who had already caught his breath.

'We need to get back to the car,' she panted.

Nick raised an eyebrow. 'Give it ten minutes. I'd rather not walk into those two again.'

'Okay,' Ruth agreed, but she was already deep in thought. The visit to the former premises of Global Escorts hadn't been as successful in giving them leads as she'd hoped. 'We have to go back to the hospital.'

'Why?'

'I need to talk to any of the girls that came back from the farmhouse,' she said as she looked at her watch. 'And I'm aware that every hour that goes by is more time for someone to arrange to get Sarah, and any of the other women, out of Paris.'

CHAPTER 15

Ruth and Nick had now spent half an hour scouring the wards of the hospital and talking to nursing staff, trying to track down the other women who had been held captive at the farmhouse in the Forêt de Sénart. Ruth was pretty sure that Vernier, along with a handful of others in the Paris Police, were the only people who knew exactly where the women were. Having seen Vernier in a conversation with Milan Golkin, she knew that seeking help from the police was no longer an option.

Ruth and Nick had narrowed their search down to a ward on the fifth floor, although the nursing staff they'd last spoken to couldn't be sure if they were still there.

A male nurse came over and asked, 'Puis-je vous aider?', which Ruth thought probably meant *Can I help you?'*

Taking out her warrant card, Ruth gave him a quizzical look. 'I don't suppose you speak any English do you?'

He laughed. 'My wife is Scottish, so yes, my English is pretty good.'

Ruth exchanged a look with Nick and smiled. *Result!*

'We're British police officers,' she explained. 'There was a police operation down in the Forêt de Sénart two days ago. I think the injured women who were found there were brought to this ward?'

'Yes, that is correct.'

'Are they still here?' Nick asked.

'No, I am afraid they all left this morning.'

Ruth felt a surge of disappointment. 'They were discharged by the doctors?'

'No.'

'I don't understand.'

'Three of them discharged themselves at the same time,' he explained.

'Isn't that unusual?' Ruth enquired.

'Very.'

'Were they fit to leave?' she asked.

'Not really.'

'Do you think they should have stayed in hospital?'

He glanced back to his colleagues a little nervously but then nodded.

'Had they had any visitors this morning?' Nick asked. 'A man in his 40s?'

The nurse gestured back to the station. 'I really think I should get back to work.'

'Please, this is important.' Ruth took out her mobile phone and showed him a photo of Milan Golkin. 'Was this the man who came to see them?'

The nurse nodded but didn't say anything.

'And then he left?' Nick asked.

'Yes.'

Ruth looked at him. 'And the women then all discharged themselves?'

'Yes. Three of them did.'

Nick rubbed his hand through his beard. 'You said three of them?'

'Yes.'

'You mean there were more than three?' Ruth asked.

'Yes, there were four.'

'Who was the fourth woman?'

'We had a young Irish woman in here.' He glanced over at his colleagues and said, 'I really should be getting back to work now.'

'What was her name?'

He blinked anxiously and whispered, 'I am not sure that I can tell you that. I have told you everything I know.'

Ruth walked up to him, glanced at his staff badge and then looked directly into his eyes. 'William. Do you have a daughter?'

He frowned. 'Yes.'

'How old is she?'

'She just turned eight.'

'It's a lovely age isn't it? I have a daughter too,' Ruth said gently. 'The women who left here today. They are all somebody's daughter, and they are all in great danger. Myself and my colleague want to find them so they can be safely returned to their families. Do you understand? This is really important.'

William blinked rapidly and thought for a few seconds. 'Yes, of course.'

He went over to the nurses' station. He grabbed a file, then came back and flicked through it. 'She said her name was Keira O'Driscoll.'

'And what happened to her?' asked Nick.

'The man that you showed me on your phone. They seemed to have some kind of argument. After he had gone, she got dressed.'

'Did she leave?' Ruth asked.

'Yes. We explained that she needed to fill out discharge papers. She swore a lot and said we were wasting her time. She also told me if the man came back to look for her, to tell him we didn't know where she had gone. Then she just walked out of here.'

'Sounds like Milan Golkin is rounding up all the women from the farmhouse,' Ruth said thinking out loud as she and Nick walked across the hospital car park. A plane flew low overhead, heading for Charles De Gaulle airport.

'Except for Keira O'Driscoll.'

Ruth pulled out a cigarette, cupped her hand against the wind, and lit it. She took a long satisfying drag.

'Whatever you say about the French, it's the one country in the world where you don't have to feel guily about smoking. In fact, they still see it as cool and chic.'

Nick gestured back to the hospital. 'Yeah, well tell that to the people lying in the oncology ward.'

'Piss off,' Ruth laughed. 'What happened to personal choice?'

Out of the corner of her eye, she spotted someone watching them. It was the young man in the bandana that she had seen at the hospital several times before. There was no doubt that he was tailing them.

'Don't look to your left, but there's a guy in a blue bandana watching us and talking into his phone,' she muttered. 'He's been at this hospital every time I've been here. I thought he was following me before, but now I'm certain.'

'Shall we go and have a word?' Nick asked.

'Why not.'

Diverting their journey back to the car, they began to weave through the parked cars towards the *bandana man* without making it obvious that they were heading his way.

He had turned away a little and seemed engrossed in the conversation he was having on the phone. He hadn't spotted them approaching.

Nick pulled out his warrant card as they got to about ten feet away. The man's eyes widened as he saw them coming towards him.

'Stay where you are!' Nick barked.

Ruth tried to reassure him. 'We just want to talk to you.'

Without hesitating, he swore in French and then took off at a sprint.

'Bollocks!' Nick growled as they began to chase him.

The man ran at full pelt along the side of the hospital towards the rear.

'Stop! Police!' Ruth bellowed as they followed him.

Bloody hell! He's fast!

He disappeared behind the back of the hospital.

Nick and Ruth followed, sprinting down a neat gravelled pathway.

By the time they reached the back of the hospital, the man had already begun to climb up onto the flat roof of a series of new Portacabins.

'Sodding hell!' Ruth cursed as she tried to get her breath.

As they reached the Portacabins, the man had already scrambled almost to the top. Ruth saw him glance back at them both. He appeared terrified.

'Stop, police!' she yelled, but he had pulled himself onto the roof and disappeared out of sight.

'Shit!' Nick growled. They had no choice but to go after him.

Ruth's heart was already thudding. Nick started to climb first, and she followed. She'd had enough of climbing and running today, and shook with the sheer effort.

'You okay?' Nick reached down from the roof to give her a helping hand.

With all dignity gone, she dismissed his outstretched hand and clambered onto the roof, grazing the skin from the palms of her hands on the rough asphalt. It stung, but she had no time to think about it.

'Never better.'

They went to the other side of the roof. Below was an open area of concrete and a series of one-storey warehouses.

The man dashed across the concrete, through an opening in some rusty, corrugated iron, and disappeared down the side of one of the warehouses.

Ruth hesitated as she looked down from the top of the Portacabin. It had to be over ten feet, and high enough for her to break her bloody ankle.

Nick jumped first, rolled onto the ground, and then stood up. 'Come on. It looks higher than it is.'

'Easy for you to say. You're down there,' she groaned. 'I'm going through the menopause and that gives you osteoporosis. I've got brittle bones.'

Nick shrugged and rolled his eyes. 'Okay, well stay there then. I'll go and get him on my own.'

Fuck it, she thought. She leapt, hit the concrete, and felt a pain shoot up the outside of her ankle.

'Ow, that really fucking hurts!' she cried out as she started to rub her ankle.

'You going to be okay?' Nick asked.

She nodded. She didn't have a choice.

'Come on,' she groaned.

They broke into a run again as Ruth gritted her teeth. Her ankle was throbbing.

They followed the route the man had taken through the gap in the corrugated iron and down the side of the warehouse.

With anger now raging, Ruth broke into a full sprint, pumping her fists as she went. She'd managed to run off the pain in her ankle.

However, the man was nowhere to be seen.

Nick slowed to a jog and gasped, 'He must have gone into one of the warehouses.'

Ruth stopped running and bent double trying to get her breath back. To her left, she looked at the lurid orange sign across the top of a giant warehouse that read *GIROUD*.

'Where the bloody hell is he?' she panted.

'Let's keep going down here, eh?' Nick suggested, motioning as they continued down the side of the enormous warehouse.

They reached a large open doorway and looked inside. The vast interior of the warehouse was about a third full of boxes and wooden pallets. There seemed to be no one around and no one working.

As they went inside, Ruth wiped her forehead on her shirt sleeve and glanced around. The air smelled of dry wood and chemicals.

Is he hiding in here? He's disappeared so it has to be worth a try.

They began to work their way through the warehouse, past towering shelves of boxes and a couple of unmanned forklift trucks. It was basically a maze and he could have gone anywhere.

A noise came from the far side of the warehouse beside a large pile of rubbish bags.

Nick and Ruth exchanged a look.

Proceeding cautiously, they weaved through the long walkways created by the boxes and made their way towards the rubbish bags.

Then a clatter. Metallic, maybe.

Another click.

What if he's got a weapon?

Ruth took a slow, quiet breath as her pulse thudded in her eardrums. She didn't want to surprise him only to get a blade shoved into her throat.

The noise stopped.

They moved closer and closer.

Suddenly, out of nowhere, two enormous pigeons flapped noisily out of the rubbish and up into the warehouse roof.

'Shit!' Ruth blurted, jumping out of her skin. 'You little fucking...'

Nick gave her a wry smile.

With a resigned sigh, Ruth wondered if they were just wasting precious time.

Then, something or someone moved about fifty yards away.

'Over there,' she whispered to Nick.

Breaking into a run, Nick sprinted in the direction in which Ruth thought the movement had come.

From behind a box, the man jumped up suddenly and made a run for it.

'Stay there!' Nick shouted, running directly at him.

Ruth broke into a jog and watched as Nick dived and took him down in a perfect rugby tackle, landing on some cardboard boxes.

By the time Ruth got to them, Nick had pulled the man to his feet and was holding his arms behind his back.

'Stay there,' Ruth snapped as she approached and got out her warrant card. 'We're British police officers.'

'I don't know nothing, man,' he muttered in an accent that was a mixture of French and Caribbean.

'Why have you been following me?' Ruth asked.

He shrugged. 'I haven't.'

Nick tightened the grip on his arms. 'We know you have.'

He grimaced and struggled a little. The restraining grip that Nick had him in was clearly uncomfortable.

Getting out her phone, Ruth quickly found a photo of Sarah and showed it to him. 'Do you know this woman?'

He looked at it briefly and then shook his head.

Nick tightened his grip. 'Why don't you look again, eh?'

He winced and then peered at the phone again. 'Yeah, I know her.'

'How?' Ruth asked.

'From the hospital.'

'Why were you at the hospital?' Nick asked.

The man shook his head.

'Who told you to go to the hospital and follow me?' Ruth demanded.

Nick twisted his arms hard and the man grimaced in pain. 'Hey, man. You can't do this to me.'

'It's all right. I'm off duty so I can do what I want.'

'Okay, okay,' he sighed after a few seconds. 'My boss. He told me to go to the hospital and check on the girls, you know?'

'Who is your boss?' Ruth asked.

'This is police brutality, man!'

Ruth stared at him defiantly. 'WHAT ... IS ... HIS ... NAME?'

After a pause, he lowered his eyes. 'His name is Ancille.'

'Where do we find him?'

'He has a club in Pigalle called *Murmure*.'

'And why does he want to know about the girls in the hospital?' Nick asked.

'I dunno,' he shrugged. 'He told me to watch them, see who they talk to and where they go.'

Ruth tapped on her phone, pulled up a photo of Milan Golkin and showed it to him. 'You know this man?'

He tensed and looked uneasy. 'Yeah.'

'Milan Golkin?'

He nodded. 'He is called the *Kayiman*. It is voodoo. In Haitian, it means the devil.'

That sounds ominous.

'Does Golkin now have all the women who were in the hospital?' Ruth asked.

'I am sorry. I don't know. Please don't hurt me. I promise you, I don't know where they are.'

Ruth looked at Nick. He let his grip go. The man turned and dashed out of the warehouse.

'Looks like we're going to Pigalle then?' Ruth said.

CHAPTER 16

Nick and Ruth parked in a side street in the Pigalle district of Paris, which ran along the border between the 9th and 18th arrondissements and was named after the famous sculptor Jean-Baptiste Pigalle. It was an area known for its neon-lit red light district with an array of sex shops and strip bars. It was also home to the infamous 19th century cabaret venue Moulin Rouge, as well as glamorous cocktail bars and chic nightclubs. To its south, the sleazy atmosphere gave way to a more upmarket environment of contemporary bistros within the neoclassical buildings of the 1800s.

Nick and Ruth weaved their way along the narrow streets, looking for *Club Murmure* which they knew lay somewhere along rue Frochot. The sex clubs were all decorated in varying shades of black, pink and gold, and offered *Cabaret Feminin* and *Table Dance.*

They soon found *Club Murmure,* which looked just as tacky as all the rest they had passed. Deciding not to wave their warrant cards immediately, they paid the €15 entry fee and went down a long, wide flight of red-carpeted stairs and into the warm darkness of the club. It smelled of cheap perfume and alcohol.

There were around thirty customers inside, watching half a dozen girls twirling around poles and dancing to the loud thudding bass of the music.

'Nice,' Ruth joked sarcastically as she gestured to the bar. 'Shall we ask over here?'

A tall woman wearing a platinum blonde wig and far too much makeup approached them and pointed over to the tables. 'Vous devez vous asseoir.'

Ruth got the gist but shook her head. 'We're looking for Ancille.'

The woman frowned and indicated they should stay where they were. 'Attends ici.'

They watched her go.

The music was so loud it was almost impossible to hear anything.

'I can't wait to tell Amanda that you made me spend my afternoon in a strip club,' Nick shouted with a grin.

Ruth rolled her eyes.

A few seconds later, the woman came back and approached them. 'Mr Ancille says he is very busy. He does not know you.'

How has he seen us to know that?

Glancing up at the ceiling, Ruth saw a black circular CCTV camera with a red flashing light.

Oh, okay, that's how.

Ruth and Nick got out their warrant cards in unison and showed them to her.

'We're British police officers,' Ruth yelled over the din of the music. 'We need to speak to Mr Ancille. Tell him it's urgent.'

The woman gave them a withering look and gestured for them to follow her. Heading across the bar, they passed through some double doors and then turned left into a dingy corridor.

The woman came to a black door, knocked, and opened it. A bald-headed man in his 50s with a neat goatee looked up at them from his desk and scowled.

'Ancille?' Ruth asked.

He tensed with annoyance. 'Who are you?'

They showed their warrant cards and his expression softened as he waved them in and shooed his employee away.

'Sit down. Would you like a drink?'

'We're fine thanks,' Ruth said.

'Okay.' He sat back in his padded chair and steepled his fingers. 'You are not French police officers then?'

'No, British,' Nick said.

'Ah, British. From London?'

Ruth shook her head. 'North Wales actually.'

'Oh, okay. It is meant to be very beautiful there.' He laughed a little too much and his eyes creased for a second. 'I understand that you met Josaphat earlier?'

'Blue bandana?' Nick asked.

'Yes. I think he might have confused things a little.'

Ruth started to speak. 'Listen, Mr Ancille ...'

'Ancille, please. It is my first name.'

'Ancille, sorry.' Ruth took out her phone. 'I'm going to cut to the chase here. I'm looking for this woman. Her name is Sarah. She is very dear to me. She was my partner, you understand?'

Ancille shrugged. 'Of course.'

'She has been held captive for the past seven years and has been forced to work as an escort for Global Escorts. You know that company?'

'Yes.'

'Sarah was freed in a police operation two days ago and taken to the Hôpital Européen Georges-Pompidou, where your friend Josaphat kept an eye on her. She was visited by this man, Milan Golkin.' Ruth showed him a photo. 'You know who he is?'

'Everyone knows Milan Golkin in this city,' he replied emphatically.

'Golkin persuaded Sarah to leave the hospital, along with three other women who had been held captive by Global Escorts. I believe that she is now being held by him somewhere in Paris.' Ruth's voice started to break a little with the exhaustion and emotion. 'I want her back. I want to take her home with me. Do you understand?'

'Yes. That is love. You want to protect her. That is natural.' Ancille stroked his goatee, as if to aid his thinking. 'This is a very difficult situation. Milan Golkin thinks of these women as possessions or assets.'

'Do you work for him?' Nick asked.

'No, no.' Ancille gave an ironic laugh. 'But when he asks me to do him a favour then I must say yes. He is not a man you say no to. Ever. Not if you want to live.'

Ruth let out a deep sigh. 'So, what do I do? I'm not leaving Paris without her.'

'You have money?' he asked.

'Some. I have savings and collateral in my home.'

'Then maybe you can buy her,' he suggested. 'This is just business to them.'

'How much?' Ruth asked, wondering whether this would work and how she could get the collateral out of her house quickly.

'I don't know, but you come here tomorrow morning and I will have an answer for you.'

Ruth and Nick travelled the short distance to Montmartre. Gus, the bar owner, had called to say he had some information but wasn't willing to talk on the phone. Parking around the corner and out of sight, they hoped they wouldn't bump into the men they had encountered earlier in the day.

As soon as Ruth and Nick walked into *Bar Chez Gus,* the proprietor got off the stool he was sitting at by the bar, stubbed out his cigarette, and beckoned them to follow him.

He led them into a cramped and untidy back office.

'Please, please, sit down,' he mumbled, gesturing to a couple of dusty chairs. He looked visibly nervous.

Ruth and Nick sat down and Gus sat on a rickety stool beside some old shelves.

'I'm sorry we have to come in here,' he whispered, his eyes blinking uneasily. 'I do not want anyone to see that I am talking to you. It is too dangerous.'

'Of course.' Ruth gave him a smile of appreciation. 'And thank you for calling me.'

'I was very fond of those girls - especially your Sarah. I hope that you can find her and take her home with you.'

Nick sat forward on his seat, which creaked a little under his weight. 'You told us that you had some information?'

'Yes, yes. One of the girls came in here about an hour ago.'

'One of the girls that worked at Global Escorts?'

'Yes.' Gus paused in thought. 'Cara. That was her name I think?'

'Do you mean Keira?' Nick suggested.

Ruth looked at him. 'Was she Irish?'

Gus nodded enthusiastically. 'Yes, yes, Irish. Beautiful red hair and freckles.'

It made sense. Keira had disappeared from the hospital and it sounded like she might be on the run.

'What did she want?' Ruth asked.

'She wanted drugs,' Gus said sadly as he shook his head, 'but the man upstairs, he is not there today. I told her to come back.'

'Anything else?' Ruth pressed, hoping that Keira could provide a clue as to the whereabouts of the other girls.

'She wanted money, but I have no money. I am an old man with a bar. She is always very charming.'

'How did she seem?' Nick asked.

Gus furrowed his brow. 'Seem? I do not understand.'

'Was she scared when she was talking to you?' Ruth clarified.

'Yes, of course. She told me there were men after her but she was trying to get out of Paris. I gave her some food and drink, and what little money I could. And then she left. I pray that she gets away from Paris. She told me once she was from Dublin.'

Ruth shifted in her chair. None of this was getting them any closer to finding Sarah, and she wasn't going to rely on Ancille and his promise to contact Golkin. For all she knew, it was just posturing and bullshit on Ancille's part.

'Did she say anything about the other girls from Global Escorts?' Nick asked.

'Yes, yes.' Gus's eyes widened. 'That is why I called you. Keira had spoken to some people she knew. She had heard that there was a plan to take all the girls out of Paris to Germany.'

'Germany?' Ruth asked. 'As far as I know, none of them have passports. Did she say how they were going to be taken to Germany?'

'Yes, she told me it was on a boat or ship.'

CHAPTER 17

It was now dark, and Ruth and Nick were sitting at a table in the rooftop bar of their hotel. They were exhausted and had sat in virtual silence for five minutes, collecting their thoughts and trying to piece together the information they had gathered.

As a warm breeze blew across Ruth's hair, she gazed out across the Paris skyline and wondered where Sarah was and if she would ever get to see her again. She couldn't bear to think of how scared she might be feeling, and feared that she was probably back taking heroin.

The Paris lights made the suburbs appear as vast fields filled with scattered stars. The sky above them might have been black, but the constellation of coloured lights gave the horizon a magical, opalescent glow.

'Penny for them,' Nick asked quietly.

She took a long swig of her wine and sighed. 'God only knows. She's out there somewhere.'

'Don't worry. We'll find her.'

'Can you get by boat from central Paris to Germany?' Ruth asked, more to herself than Nick.

'I guess so, if you use the right canals and rivers. A friend of mine reckons you could travel all the way from Wales to the Mediterranean in a boat, using the rivers and canals.'

'What about the English Channel?'

'Yeah, well Kevin's not the brightest spark on the planet.'

A smile tugged at her lips. 'Maybe that's what they're planning then?'

'If they don't have passports, and they have the French authorities looking for them, then I guess using European backwaters to move around would make perfect sense.'

'Evening,' a voice said. 'Traffic was terrible, as is my time-keeping.'

It was Trelford, whom Ruth had arranged to meet for a quick update.

'Hi Oliver,' she mumbled wearily.

Trelford could see the stress in her eyes. 'Gosh. You really have had a day of it. Can I get anyone a drink?'

'Thanks, but we're fine, Oliver. Come and sit down.'

Trelford pulled up a chair. 'Not very much my end, I'm afraid. I have spoken to the Paris Police now and they're aware that several of the girls from Global Escorts have discharged themselves from hospital. However, as with Sarah, they haven't committed a crime by leaving. They are interested in the girls as witnesses but there is no urgency to find them because they don't believe they are in danger.'

Nick felt a flicker of irritation. 'But they're victims of modern slavery, kidnapping, trafficking, assault, you name it,' he said incredulously.

'Yes, that's all true,' Trelford agreed, 'and they're vital witnesses against those behind Global Escorts. But you know, as I do, some of Global Escorts' clientele were very rich, powerful men in French society.'

'The Paris Police department?' Ruth asked.

'If you believe the rumours, then yes.' He considered for a moment, then added, 'And judges, politicians, film stars, footballers ...'

'So, no one is willing to try and stop these women from being trafficked out of Paris?' Ruth blurted, not hiding her anger.

Trelford noted her tone and sat back a little in his chair. 'Everyone will tell you that they are doing all they can to find them, but the reality is that no one really has the appetite for the horrendous can of worms that would be unearthed if these women started to name names. There are many who are praying that the women disappear and the whole problem goes away.'

Ruth shook her head in exasperation. Even as an experienced police officer, she couldn't believe that a city like Paris, in a major European country, actually worked in this way.

'For fuck's sake!' she said in a raised voice. 'How can we be in a place where a high-ranking Paris detective is seen talking to a Russian assassin and no one seems particularly surprised!'

'I don't know,' Trelford admitted, 'but we have to work on the premise that we can't trust anyone.'

'What about the DGSE?'

Trelford rubbed the back of his neck. 'I've heard very good things about Camille Moreau. But the more people you involve, the more likely it is that someone somewhere will find out what you're doing and try to stop you.'

Nick looked at Ruth. 'Makes sense.'

'You said that there had been a few developments?' Trelford directed his question to Ruth.

'Yes. I'm just paranoid about who might be listening in to my calls. I thought it would be safer to do this face to face.'

'Of course.'

'One of the Global Escorts workers, an Irish woman named Keira O'Driscoll, did a runner from the hospital and, as far as we know, Milan Golkin is still looking for her.'

Nick leant forward on his chair. 'Effectively, she's on the run and trying to get out of Paris.'

'Have you made contact with her?' Trelford asked.

Ruth shook her head. 'No. There's a bar opposite the old premises of Global Escorts in Montmartre. Bar Chez Gus. The girls used to score drugs in the flat above and then go and sit in the bar drinking and chatting. Keira O'Driscoll turned up there earlier today looking to score.'

'What happened?'

'The drug dealer wasn't there but the proprietor, Gus, gave her food and some money,' Nick replied.

Ruth lowered her voice and said, 'Keira claimed she had heard that Golkin was taking the girls he had recaptured out of Paris to Germany by boat.'

'By boat? How does that work?'

'We're assuming that if you use canals and rivers, you can eventually navigate your way from Paris to Germany.'

'I guess you can,' Trelford agreed, 'and without passports, and the authorities supposedly looking for Golkin and these women, they can't just waltz onto a plane or a ferry.'

'That was our thinking,' Nick said.

'Can you look at Interpol's records and see if anything comes up in terms of boat ownership for Global Escorts or any-one connected to them?' Ruth asked him.

'Of course. Nothing rings a bell but I'll have a look. You mentioned that you'd been to a club? Is that right?'

'*Club Murmure* in Pigalle,' Nick informed him.

'Murmure? Sounds lovely. I haven't heard of it.'

Nick inclined his head slightly and smiled. 'I don't think it's your kind of place, Oliver.'

'It's owned by a man named Ancille. I'm pretty sure he's North African,' Ruth added.

Trelford thought for a moment. 'He's not someone I've come across,' he said eventually.

Nick locked eyes with him. 'Golkin paid him to keep an eye on the girls while they were in hospital. Which ward they were on, who they were talking to, that kind of thing.'

Trelford seemed surprised. 'And he told you all this, did he?'

'Yes, he seemed fairly blasé about the whole thing,' Ruth continued. 'I asked him to find out if I could buy Sarah back from Golkin.'

'What?' Trelford's eyes widened.

Ruth shrugged. 'They see the women as commodities. And every commodity has a price.'

Trelford's expression changed. 'Aren't you forgetting something?'

'What?' Ruth asked. His tone and expression had made her feel uneasy.

'Sarah knows too much about Global Escorts and their clients,' he warned. 'I really don't think they would be interested in any kind of deal with her knowing all that.'

Ruth and Nick exchanged a look. Trelford was probably right, and Ruth felt naïve for getting her hopes up.

CHAPTER 18

It was early morning. Ruth and Nick were back in Pigalle to meet Ancille and find out if he'd had any contact with Milan Golkin overnight. Ruth knew it was a long shot, but they were running out of time and options. She wondered if Ancille might know anything about a boat.

As they approached the club, the road was being washed down by city council workers. The atmosphere was noisy and smelly, in stark contrast to the enticingly sleazy, neon-lit Pigalle at night.

The tall woman they had encountered yesterday was crouching down on the pavement, unlocking the shutters at the entrance to *Club Murmure*.

Ruth wondered if she might recognise them. 'Bonjour. We were here yesterday?'

The woman's gaze flicked briefly from Ruth to Nick and ended in a glare, as if to say *So what*?

'Oui?' she snapped as she shoved the shutters up and they rose with a noisy metallic clank.

Nick smirked at her rudeness. 'We've come to see Ancille.'

'Is he here?' Ruth asked.

She gestured with her arms in annoyance. 'Oui, oui. Entrer! Entrer!'

Nick smiled at Ruth. 'I think she wants us to go in.'

'What gave you that idea?' Ruth said facetiously.

They walked down the staircase and into the deserted and silent club.

Nick grimaced. 'It's even worse in the daylight when it's empty.'

'Don't pretend that you haven't been to places like this before.'

'Yeah, but not for a very long time.'

They followed the same route as the day before and headed for Ancille's office.

Ruth was preoccupied by what Trelford had told her the previous evening - that Golkin wouldn't trade Sarah because she knew too much. It was obvious when she thought about it. Her desire and desperation to get Sarah back had clouded her judgement. However, there was part of her that clung on to the hope that Golkin might be willing to sell Sarah if the sum of money was large enough. She had savings, plus collateral in the house if she needed to raise the funds.

As they approached Ancille's office, Ruth noticed that the door was wide open.

Good. Looks like he's definitely in.

She paused at the door, surveying the scene in front of her.

'Shit!' she mumbled, turning back to Nick. The place had been ransacked.

'This isn't good,' he whispered, glancing around at the mess.

Ruth proceeded cautiously through the door, stepping over the smashed furniture and scattered paperwork. The office had been trashed but Ancille was nowhere to be seen. If he had been attacked, the intruders might still be nearby.

Behind her, Nick picked up a piece of broken wood from the floor and held it like a weapon, ready for action.

Ruth could feel her pulse thudding in her neck. She took a deep breath and readied herself as they went back out into the corridor.

'Ancille?' she called out, as she and Nick proceeded carefully along the shadowy corridor that led to more rooms and offices.

They stopped and listened.

Nothing.

Ruth glanced at Nick. She tilted her head slightly and raised an eyebrow, a well-rehearsed gesture to query whether he had heard anything. He shook his head.

They came to a larger office further along. It had also been ransacked. Nick crouched down to inspect the objects and papers that were littered all over the floor.

'I'll check the other rooms,' Ruth whispered quietly as she went slowly down the corridor.

'Be careful,' Nick warned.

She opened the door to a small bedroom that was clearly used by prostitutes. The stained mattress had been propped against the wall. On the other side of the room, there was an open door that led to a dark bathroom. She walked over and peered in. There was nothing out of the ordinary and the shower curtain had been pulled across the bath.

'Anything?' Nick called out.

'No ... Where the hell is Ancille then?' Ruth muttered under her breath.

She turned and headed out of the bedroom and back into the darkness of the corridor.

Nick approached holding a framed photograph which had been smashed. It featured a photograph of Ancille in a restaurant shaking hands with a man and holding up a glass of wine. It was Patrice Le Bon.

There was a noise from somewhere behind her. It was either a movement or a groan.

'What the bloody hell was that?'

'Someone in there?' Nick suggested as he pointed to the bedroom she had been in.

'I thought I'd checked in there,' she said with a frown as they made their way back towards the bedroom.

She reached the bathroom before Nick.

It sounded like the noise had come from there.

She glanced in the mirror and spotted something she hadn't seen in the darkness the first time.

The reflection of a bloody smear across the white tiles of the wall behind the shower curtain.

Oh my God!

'In here,' Ruth whispered quietly. Bracing herself, she pulled back the shower curtain slowly.

A man's body, drenched in blood, was laying in the bath. Lifeless grey eyes, wide open with fear, were staring up at her.

It was Ancille.

Nick took a step back. 'Jesus Christ!'

'Bloody hell!' Ruth gasped looking at his blood-soaked clothes and hair. His throat had been cut from ear to ear.

Suddenly, a man holding a pistol appeared at the bedroom door. The barrel of the gun was aimed right at Ruth's face.

'Restez où vous etes!'

Oh shit, he's going to shoot us.

Nick raised his hands in a gesture of surrender. 'It's all right,' he said softly, 'take it nice and easy, mate.'

As the man moved out of the shadows and into the room, they could see that he was a French police officer wearing a dark blue uniform.

'Shit! He's a copper,' Ruth gasped with some relief.

'Ne bougez pas!' he shouted.

'It's okay,' Ruth said calmly, 'we're British police officers.' She turned to Nick. 'What's police in French?'

'No idea,' he replied.

The officer waved the pistol at them to indicate he wanted them outside in the corridor.

'Ils sont ici!' he shouted, and out of nowhere more armed French police stormed down the corridor.

'Detective Inspector Hunter?' asked a voice.

A figure strolled into view from out of the darkness.

It was Vernier.

This is not good.

'We've just found a man murdered in there,' Ruth announced, indicating the bedroom and bathroom behind her.

Vernier walked in, went to the bathroom, saw the body and returned.

'Who is he?' he asked, showing n0 emotion.

Ruth was feeling very uneasy. She had seen Vernier talking to Golkin. That meant Vernier was corrupt, and probably being paid off by Le Bon. Did that mean that Ruth and Nick were going to get gunned down right here and now? Or did it mean they were going to be taken away and mysteriously disappear? Whatever happened, she knew that she couldn't trust a word that Vernier said.

'He's the club owner, Ancille,' Nick responded.

'Ancille?' Vernier turned his attention to Ruth. 'How do you know a club owner in Pigalle, Detective?'

Ruth's heart was pounding in her chest. 'I don't. I really don't. I think he works for Milan Golkin, that's all I know.'

She wasn't about to tell Vernier any more than that.

'Golkin is a very dangerous man,' he warned. Then he raised an eyebrow. 'So, you came to see this man today and you just found him lying in the bath with his throat cut?'

'Yes,' Ruth confirmed.

'Did you see anyone when you got here?'

'No.'

'No one suspicious? No one hanging around or leaving the premises?'

'No.'

Vernier stiffened, his jaw tensing. 'That seems strange, doesn't it?'

'I suppose so,' Ruth snapped. 'You sound like you don't believe us.'

'I don't believe you Detective Inspector.'

'Why not?'

'Because you will do anything to get your friend Sarah back. You're not telling me everything you know. You're at the scene of this murder with no explanation. And you're wasting my time.'

Ruth stared at him, outraged. 'This is ridiculous!'

Vernier looked at the other officers and gestured to Ruth and Nick. 'Les Arrêter!'

'What?' Nick thundered.

Two uniformed officers unclipped the handcuffs from their belts, came over and started to cuff them.

'You can't do this!' Ruth yelled.

Vernier fixed her with an icy stare. 'Yes, I can.'

CHAPTER 19

Ruth and Nick were sitting in an interview room in the La Préfecture, on the Île de la Cité in the centre of the city. Their handcuffs had been removed as soon as they had arrived. It had clearly been Vernier's attempt to scare them. He sat behind his desk with a large mug of coffee and some paperwork.

'You're not leaving me very much choice,' he grumbled eventually.

'What does that mean?' Ruth asked. She didn't have time for his bullshit. For all she knew, Sarah might be on a boat on the Seine waiting to be taken away. Surely they weren't going to be charged with anything? They hadn't committed a crime, for God's sake! However, from what she had learnt of the Paris Police, she wasn't certain that mattered.

'You are interfering with a police investigation in a city where you have no legal jurisdiction,' he snapped at her. 'In fact, you're not here in any official capacity at all.'

'What police investigation?' she said accusingly. 'You managed to botch up an operation to rescue twelve women who had been trafficked. You allowed any evidence to be destroyed, and several of those women are back in the hands of their captors. They're hardly going to give you a medal!'

Anger flashed across his face. 'It is none of your business how I run the investigations in this department.'

Nick's eyes bored into his. 'You're not running an investigation. You're sitting on your hands and allowing vulnerable trafficked women to be taken out of your city!'

'No,' Vernier cut in sharply, 'this is part of a wider investigation which neither of you have any knowledge of. I will not have you two running around showing your British police identification and conducting your own investigation. A complaint has been registered with both your Home Office and the North Wales Police.'

'Good!' Ruth said emphatically. 'Good. I'm happy to explain exactly what is going on to both of them.'

Vernier took a long swig of his coffee. 'Then you'll have to do that when you get back home.'

Ruth fixed him with a glare. 'We're not going home.'

'I'm afraid you are. It has been arranged.' He pointed to the file in front of him. 'I have all the paperwork here.'

Ruth shifted forward in her chair. 'What bloody paperwork?'

'Tomorrow morning you will be escorted onto a flight from Charles De Gaulle airport to Manchester by my officers.'

Nick's shoulders rose defensively. 'This is a bloody joke!'

'Now, you have a choice,' Vernier explained coldly. 'You can spend the night here, in a room like this. Or you can be escorted back to your hotel, where you will stay until you are picked up in the morning.'

Ruth looked at Nick. 'We'll go to the hotel.'

'Don't worry. I will have men outside to make sure that you don't leave. You are effectively now under house arrest,' he said dismissively.

Ruth and Nick had been back in Ruth's hotel room for half an hour. There was no way that they were going to stay put. She had left a message for Trelford but she knew Interpol had no real power.

Nick had opened the main window in the room and was looking out to see if there were any fire escapes they could use to leave the hotel and avoid detection.

'Anything?' Ruth asked hopefully.

Nick shook his head. 'Not unless you're Spiderman.'

Ruth's phone rang. It was Moreau.

'Camille?'

'Ruth, I'm guessing you're still in Paris?' she asked.

'Yes. Unfortunately we seem to have found ourselves under house arrest by the Paris Police. We're being escorted to the airport tomorrow and flown home.'

'I'm sorry to hear that,' Moreau said. 'I'm assuming you tried to find Golkin?'

'Yes, and while I'm upright and breathing, I'm not going home without Sarah.'

Moreau gave a little laugh. 'I admire your courage, Ruth.'

'Thank you.'

'I think that you are a little bit crazy, but also very brave. I have something for you, but it might be too late. We have a source who tells us that Sarah and the other women that have been recaptured are on a boat on the Seine,' Moreau informed her.

Ruth nodded to herself. 'That confirms what we heard.'

Moreau continued, 'Our source tells us that the boat is leaving Paris at ten o'clock tonight.'

Ruth glanced at her watch. Her heart sank - it was 8.22pm. 'That gives us less than two hours. Do you know anything else about the boat? Its name, what it looks like or where it's moored?'

'I'm sorry, no. That's all I have. It would seem that you are going to be too late to save her.'

'Well we'll see about that,' Ruth said with determination.

'Let me know how things go Ruth, and bonne chance.'

The call ended.

Nick looked at her uncertainly. 'What's going on?'

'The boat carrying Sarah leaves at ten.'

He glanced at his watch and gave a sigh of frustration. 'How do we get out of this bloody hotel?'

Then Ruth had an idea. 'The roof.'

'What do you mean?'

'Maybe we can leave the hotel from the rooftop bar.'

CHAPTER 20

Ten minutes later Ruth and Nick sauntered into the rooftop bar, trying not to attract any undue attention. The soft light from the strings of ornate bulbs that criss-crossed and decorated the terrace meant that it was difficult to see anyone clearly. The sloping cream-coloured awnings gave them even more cover as they weaved between the tables. Ruth assumed that Vernier had only stationed his men outside the hotel to check that they didn't leave, and not to actually spy on them elsewhere in the hotel.

They walked over to the far end of the rooftop bar which was marked by a three-foot high white stone balustrade and some thick, potted coniferous plants. Ruth's instincts had been right. In the darkness, it looked as though the roofs of the adjacent buildings were all connected at the same level. Essentially they should be able to walk along the flat rooftops until they found another way down the nine floors to the ground.

Glancing around to make sure no one was watching, Nick took out his phone and turned on the light. He stepped over the balustrade and shone his phone to have a look.

'Oh shit!' He turned back to look at her. 'Good news and bad news.'

'Good news?' Ruth asked.

'We can definitely get to the roof of the building next door.'

'So, what's the bad news?'

Nick pointed over his shoulder. 'There's a very small gap between the two buildings which we'll have to jump.'

Ruth hated heights at the best of times. 'When you say very small ...?'

'Four feet, maybe five,' Nick said. 'It's not far to jump.'

'Easy for you to say,' she groaned. 'And if I don't manage to jump across the gap?'

Nick winced. 'Yeah, it's a hundred foot drop to the bottom.'

'Oh good,' she joked sardonically and then looked at her watch. 'Well fuck it. We don't have time to piss about do we?'

'Not really, no. It's going to have to be a standing jump, which does technically make it more difficult.'

Ruth climbed over the balustrade and looked across the gap. Even though she knew it really was only four or five feet, it seemed an enormous distance to her. And if she didn't reach the other side, she would die.

Jesus! Don't look down. And don't die!

Nick touched her forearm lightly. 'I'll go first, in case I need to help you across.'

She watched as he took a step back and prepared himself. He then sprang forward and leapt across the space with a single bound.

Turning around, he gave her an impish smile and held out his hand. 'Piece of piss. Now your turn.'

Ruth felt sick to her stomach as she looked out across the rooftops.

I can't do this without a run-up or I'm going to plummet down there!

A little to her right she noticed a small gap in the balustrade, presumably for access. She took a deep breath and walked towards it, relieved that she now had a clear run-up.

'Come on. You're going to be fine,' Nick shouted over.

Without a moment's more thought, she took off at a full sprint, planted her foot on the edge of the hotel roof and jumped into the darkness.

Time seemed to stand still.

Even though she had told herself not to look down, she couldn't help herself.

Below was a deep chasm of blackness.

She hit the roof on the other side and rolled onto its gritty surface. Looking up, she saw Nick grinning down and holding out his hand. 'See? Told you. Piece of piss.'

'I think my heart is going to burst out of my chest!' she panted as she got to her feet.

As they began to walk carefully across the flat roof, Ruth's phone rang.

It was a Paris phone number which she recognised. Gus.

'Gus? Everything okay?' she asked.

'Yes,' he whispered. 'Keira is back. She is talking about the boat that you were asking me about.'

'Can you keep her there?'

'I will do my best, but please hurry if you wish to speak to her,' Gus warned her.

CHAPTER 21

By 8.50pm, Ruth and Nick had made their way across the next two roofs and found themselves in the rooftop garden of an apartment block. From there, it was a simple walk down nine flights of stairs to the ground floor – and out of sight of Vernier's men. With the hire car parked outside the front of their hotel, they were forced to head for Bar Chez Gus on foot. It was less than half a mile and they got there after a five-minute jog. They were both aware that the clock was ticking.

As they approached the bar, they saw customers sitting outside drinking, smoking and laughing. Gus appeared from a side door. He was carrying a crate of empty bottles which he loaded into an old battered Renault Alaskan pickup truck. When he saw them approaching, he immediately looked concerned and beckoned them over.

'Where is she?' Ruth asked quietly.

Gus gestured inside. 'Sitting at the bar, but she is very nervous. I don't know if she'll talk to you. Please do not scare her.'

'Of course.' Ruth nodded with a benign expression. 'Thank you.'

Walking into the warmth of the bar, Ruth spotted an attractive woman in her mid-20s with wavy auburn hair sitting at the bar nursing a beer. Nick nodded to confirm he had seen her too.

'You go first,' he whispered.

Walking slowly over to the bar, Ruth pulled out a stool that was about three feet away from where Keira was sitting. She sat down and looked over at her furtively.

Keira sipped her beer but was aware of Ruth's gaze. She turned and looked at her. 'Well I can tell you're not French,' she joked in a thick Irish accent.

Ruth smiled. 'Oh dear. Is it that obvious?'

'Londoner, at a guess?'

'Spot on.'

'Have we met before somewhere?'

Ruth shook her head. 'No. But I'm a friend of Sarah's.'

Keira looked blank. 'Sarah. I don't know any Sarah.'

'Yes, you do,' Ruth told her quietly. 'Sarah Goddard? Or you might have known her as Amandine Thiney?'

The penny dropped and Keira immediately looked spooked. She shifted uncomfortably on her stool and moved her bag, which was on the bar, closer to her.

'Who are you?' she asked, looking as if she was already thinking of doing a runner.

Ruth put up her hands in a friendly gesture. 'Please don't run. My name is Ruth. I'm a very good friend of Sarah's. I was there when you were all rescued from the farmhouse three days ago. I was in the hospital with Sarah yesterday.'

Keira's face dropped as she got off her stool and gathered up her bag. 'Which means you're a copper? I don't like or trust coppers.'

Shit! She's going to run out of here.

Keira turned to head for the door.

'I am a copper in Wales,' Ruth admitted, 'but not here. I was Sarah's partner when she went missing seven years ago. I came to Paris to take her home with me.'

Keira looked at her for a few seconds and then put her bag back down on the bar. 'Seriously?'

'Seriously. I hadn't seen her for over seven years until three days ago. And now she's been taken again and I just need to find her.'

A frown creased Keira's brow. 'Did Gus tell you I was here?'

'Yes, he rang me. He thought that you might be able to help me find Sarah before it's too late.'

Keira paused. 'Got any cigarettes?' she asked finally.

Ruth patted her jacket pocket. 'Yes.'

Keira gestured to an empty table out on the pavement. 'We'll sit out there then so we can smoke.'

'Sounds like a plan,' Ruth agreed. They went outside and sat at the empty table. Keira looked over at Nick.

'Who's he then?'

'Just a friend who's come out here to help me find Sarah.'

'Copper too, is he?'

'Yes.'

Ruth glanced down at her watch. It was 9.10pm, which meant it was only 50 minutes before the boat was due to leave Paris. Time was tight, but she didn't want to rush Keira if she had vital information for them.

'Here you go,' Ruth said, offering her a cigarette from the packet.

'Cheers,' Keira mumbled as she took it with trembling hands.

Ruth gave her a light, then lit her own, took a drag and blew out a plume of smoke. 'That's better.'

Keira smiled. 'I know where Sarah is.'

Ruth held her breath. 'Okay.'

'There's a boat on the Seine. It belongs to Patrice Le Bon,' she began.

There was a strange buzzing sound coming from behind Ruth that was getting louder and louder.

What the hell is that?

Gus arrived at their table and smiled. 'Can I get you ladies a drink on the house?'

Suddenly, a black scooter pulled up on the pavement beside them.

Both the rider and passenger were wearing blacked-out helmets, bomber jackets and jeans.

Before Ruth could react, the passenger pulled out a handgun, aimed it at them and started shooting.

CRACK! CRACK! CRACK!

Diving across the table, she pushed Keira off her seat and they both landed on the ground.

Jesus!

CRACK! CRACK! CRACK!

'Stay down!' Ruth shouted as they huddled for cover under the table.

There were shouts and screams as the scooter sped away into the darkness.

'Are you okay?' Nick yelled as he arrived and pulled the upturned table away.

'I think so,' Ruth whimpered, getting to her feet and wiping fragments of broken glass off her. She couldn't feel anything that would suggest she had been shot.

A figure lay sprawled on the pavement.

It was Gus.

Oh my God! No!

He had a bullet hole in his forehead.

His eyes were open but he was dead.

Nick's features were blanched in sorrow. 'Jesus ...' he said quietly.

Ruth looked around but couldn't see Keira anywhere. Had she been shot? Where the hell was she?

'Where is Keira?' she cried out frantically. Keira had just revealed she knew where Sarah was and now she had disappeared.

'Down there!' Nick shouted, pointing down the road.

Keira was running away from the bar towards the line of parked scooters. She stopped, pulled one of the scooters free from where it was resting, threw her leg over the seat and started the engine.

'Shit! She can't get away!' Ruth screamed.

The sound of a siren was getting closer. The police were on their way.

Nick turned, ran over to Gus's body, reached inside his trouser pocket, and pulled out a bunch of keys. He held them up to Ruth and then pointed to the old Renault Alaskan parked outside the bar.

'Come on!' he shouted, knowing there was nothing they could do to help Gus.

She sprinted over and jumped in.

As she looked up, she could see the red tail lights of Keira's scooter snaking away down the road and into the traffic.

'She knows where Sarah is,' Ruth gasped.

Nick turned the ignition and hit the accelerator, spinning the wheels as they set off in pursuit.

Rage pulsed through his veins as he thought of Gus' needless death. 'Don't worry, I'm on it.'

CHAPTER 22

As they hurtled down rue Houdon, Nick rapidly built up speed and hit 50kph in just a few seconds. Ruth gripped the door handle with one hand and the dashboard in front with the other as the pickup screamed around a bend.

She couldn't see Keira's scooter anywhere.

'Shit! Please tell me we haven't lost her!'

'Not if I've got anything to do with it,' Nick said through clenched teeth.

As they sped south across the city, they hammered across Place de Jean-Baptiste Pigalle and headed the wrong way down a one way street. Cyclists and pedestrians scattered as Nick swerved to avoid a bus.

'Jesus!' he muttered.

Ruth sat forwards a little, peering through the windscreen. 'Where are you, Keira, where are you?'

As they tore down rue Jean-Baptiste Pigalle, the red tail light of Keira's scooter came into view, speeding up a hill a few hundred yards ahead.

'I think that's her!' Ruth glanced at her watch. It was 09.40 pm.

'How long have we got?' Nick asked.

'Twenty minutes before the boat leaves, except we don't know what it's called, where it is, or what it looks like.'

Nick gestured to Keira's scooter up ahead. 'Then we'd better find a way of stopping her before she gets away.'

Ruth felt the pickup's back tyres losing grip and slipping as they cornered another bend.

She took a quick look at Nick. 'Or before one of us gets killed in this thing.'

Nick went hammering along a narrow road. As they hurtled past tables and diners on the pavements it seemed to Ruth that they were only missing them by inches.

Keira's scooter was now only about two hundred yards ahead, so they were gaining on her.

The road narrowed again with hardly any space between the parked cars to the left and the buildings on the right.

A cyclist appeared out of nowhere.

Nick swerved left to avoid the cyclist but smashed a series of wing mirrors clean off the parked cars.

'Bloody hell!'

'What are we going to do when we catch up with her?' Ruth asked breathlessly.

'Good question. I haven't worked that bit out yet.'

'Which direction are we going?' The boat was leaving from the Seine so Ruth was praying they were heading the right way.

'South.'

'Is that good?'

'We're heading for central Paris and the Seine, if that's what you mean?' he answered.

'Yes.'

He continued. 'Although even if we can narrow down the boat to the centre, I'm guessing we'll still have five or six miles of river to check.'

Ruth didn't reply. She had the overwhelming feeling that the odds were stacking up against them getting to Sarah in time, let alone rescuing her.

'I don't think we're going to make it,' she said despondently.

'You can't think like that,' Nick said with a steely determination, dropping the car into third as they reached a long stretch of road.

Ruth knew that Keira wouldn't stop now. She'd be too scared after the shooting at the bar.

They screamed across rue Sant-Lazare and screeched round a bend beyond. They were going so fast that Ruth felt they were going to plough into a car or a building at any second.

Just up ahead, a minibus pulled out of a side road in front of them. Nick steered the car onto the opposite side of the road, missing it by a few feet.

'For God's sake!' he bellowed.

Ruth thought that she didn't want to die today, and closed her eyes as they careered around another bend. She opened them as another car flashed past.

Keira's scooter was now only a hundred yards away. It pulled out to overtake a short line of stationary traffic. Nick had no choice but to do the same. A huge articulated lorry was coming the other way. Ruth's eyes widened with alarm – there just wasn't enough time or space to get past. Nick dropped down into third gear and the pickup roared uncomfortably, but the boost in speed bought them a couple of extra seconds and they made it past with inches to spare.

'Shit!' Nick stared fiercely ahead at the scooter, which was now only fifty yards in front of them.

'Just don't lose her! Please!'

'If I get any closer, I'm going to hit her,' he said.

They came to the enormous Place de la Concord, with its confusing intersection of roads, cobbled pedestrian walkways, and countless historic statues.

Keira veered her scooter up onto the pavement in order to cut straight across the huge square. Nick followed, sending pedestrians running for their lives.

'Oh my God!' Ruth shrieked.

A few seconds later, they followed her down onto Port de la Concorde.

Even though it was dark, she could see the River Seine was immediately to their left as they hammered along its bank, with the lights of the Eiffel Tower in the distance on the other side of the river.

Suddenly, a taxi pulled out in front of them.

Keira's lights glared bright red as she slammed on her brakes.

'Bloody hell!' Nick shouted, as he hit his own brakes with full force and the vehicle started to skid.

As Ruth glanced ahead she saw that Keira had lost her balance, and she and her scooter were now sliding along the road surface completely out of control.

The pickup slid sideways and bounced off the riverside railings. The impact threw Ruth forwards and she closed her eyes. The scraping of metal against metal, the sound of cracking glass. After a few more seconds they came to a stop.

She blinked open her eyes and immediately looked over at Nick. Blood was running from his nose.

'You okay?'

He turned his head towards her and exhaled a deep breath. 'I think so.'

He tried his door but it wouldn't open. It had been damaged in the blow against the railings. Through their shattered windscreen, Ruth saw people gathering around a figure lying in the middle of the road.

'Keira!' she screamed.

She threw open the passenger door and got out, gripping the top of the door with both hands in an effort to steady herself. Nick eased himself over the gear stick onto the passenger seat and then scrambled out.

Without speaking, they both sprinted towards where Keira was lying. Black smoke was billowing from the scooter.

Ruth got there first. She could instantly smell the petrol that had spilled from the shattered remains of the scooter. She crouched down and looked at Keira. She was unconscious and her face was covered in blood.

'Get back. There's petrol everywhere,' she warned the concerned onlookers, while frantically tugging Keira away from the middle of the road and the burning scooter.

She reached a small grassy bank and put Keira in the recovery position as Nick approached.

Suddenly, the fuel ignited across the road. *Vump!* A ball of orange and yellow flames mushroomed up into the dark sky, followed by thick black smoke as the scooter crackled with flames.

Ruth began to sob.

'How is she?' Nick asked.

'She's alive, but she's unconscious.'

A young couple bolted towards them, their faces filled with shock.

'We're here on holiday,' blurted a woman in her 20s with an American accent. 'My husband is a doctor and we saw what happened. He should take a look at her.'

Ruth nodded gratefully.

The young man crouched down and began to check Keira. 'What's her name?'

'Keira. Her name's Keira,' Ruth said desperately.

'Keira ... Keira ... can you hear me? My name's Tom and I'm a doctor.'

He continued to check her over.

'Is she going to be okay?' Nick asked.

The young doctor looked up. 'Breathing and pulse are fine but she's unconscious. We need paramedics here urgently.'

There was a burst of lights and a siren as an ambulance drew up beside them. The growing crowd of onlookers moved out of the way.

The paramedics jumped out and began to examine Keira as they spoke in broken English to the young American doctor.

'Looks like she's in good hands now,' Nick said.

Ruth stood up, turned and looked out over the darkness of the Seine. She checked her watch. It was 10.06 pm.

Her heart sank and tears welled in her eyes.

'Come on,' Nick urged, 'we're on the Seine so we can find the boat.'

All the fight and hope had drained out of Ruth. She had an overwhelming sense that she and Sarah were destined to be apart.

'It's too late, Nick,' she whispered as she wiped the tears away, 'she's gone.'

Nick put his hands on her shoulders and looked at her with determination. 'We can't give up now.'

'The boat left at ten,' she sighed as she gestured to the Seine in front of them, 'and we've got over five miles of river to search. It's over, Nick.'

CHAPTER 23

They moved towards the railings, and for a brief moment they just stared out at the river and the bank beyond which was bathed in a vanilla glow from the Parisienne street lights.

A long white boat appeared from under a bridge. It was full of tourists taking photographs, and had the words *Bateaux Parisiene* painted on its side.

'There must be something that someone can do,' Nick insisted. 'What about the DGSE?'

'We don't even know what boat we're looking for,' Ruth murmured, her tears just a breath away. 'There are hundreds. Imagine the manpower and resources needed to try and search every boat travelling up and down the Seine tonight.'

'I can't believe that's it.' Nick puffed out his cheeks and exhaled.

Ruth dropped her gaze. 'Neither can I.'

He put a reassuring arm around her shoulders. 'I'm so sorry, Ruth.'

Moving closer to the railings, she took a deep breath as the sound of water lapping against the stone embankment grew louder.

Another boat was travelling the other way down the Seine. There was the thudding bass of a disco and bright technicolour flashing lights. Partygoers were waving over at them and whooping, hollering and laughing.

Ruth felt crushed.

Just as the party boat disappeared under the bridge, another expensive-looking white boat came the other way.

On its side was written the word *Celestine*.

Ruth stared in disbelief. 'What was the name that was scribbled on that piece of paper that we found at Global Escorts?'

'Celestine, wasn't it? Why?'

With her heart beginning to race, she pointed to the boat drifting past them – *Celestine*.

'Oh my God, that could be it, couldn't it?'

'Yes,' Ruth cried, pulling him by his arm. 'Come on.'

They turned and sprinted along the embankment east towards the next bridge over the river which was about 500 yards away.

The embankment was lined by a variety of houseboats, all moored in a single line. Owners, who were sitting out on deck with drinks, looked over as they ran past at full pelt.

Ruth's phone rang. Even though she was sprinting, instinct told her to check who was calling. It was Trelford.

She clicked the button as she ran. 'Oliver, we think we've found the boat,' she said breathlessly.

'It's called the Celestine,' he confirmed.

'What?'

'I've just heard from an informant that the boat is called the Celestine.'

'Thanks,' she gasped. 'That's what I thought.'

She hung up.

The bridge was now only about two hundred yards away but the boat was starting to pass them on the river.

No!

'It's definitely that boat!' she called over to Nick.

Up ahead, she could see that the roadway they were on passed through a tunnel alongside the main span of the bridge. Above that was a brightly-lit historic statue of a horse and its rider.

A sweeping set of stone steps to the right of them clearly led up to the bridge itself.

Clattering up the steps to the top, Ruth could feel every muscle in her body burning with the buildup of lactic acid.

Turning right, they thundered across to the middle of the bridge.

Nick looked down at the river which was about twenty feet below. 'Are we actually jumping down from here?'

'Have you got a better idea?' Ruth shouted back.

'No!'

As the *Celestine* approached, Ruth climbed up onto the ornate stone balustrade at the edge of the bridge and watched as the boat started to pass underneath.

She stood with her arms out a little to steady herself.

The black water below her looked terrifying.

Jesus! I can't believe we're doing this!

As the wind picked up and swirled around her, she almost lost her balance.

Please God, don't let me fall into the water.

A second later, the rear deck of the boat was directly below her.

She took a long, deep breath.

Fuck it! Here we go!

With her eyes barely open, she stepped off the bridge. A second later, she crashed onto the wooden deck and rolled over. It knocked the wind out of her. She heard a thud and saw that Nick had done the same.

For a moment or two, Ruth sat blinking and trying to get her breath back. She had banged her knee but other than that she seemed to be intact.

'You okay?' Nick asked quietly as he scuttled across the deck towards her.

'Yeah, never better,' she wheezed as she picked herself up.

They moved quickly and hid behind a metal stairway.

Suddenly there was a noise.

A steel door on the other side of the deck began to open. A blonde man with a hand-held radio appeared and looked around. He scowled and went back inside.

Ruth's heart was thumping in her chest as she tried to get her bearings.

'Stay where you are!' snapped a voice from behind them in an Eastern European accent.

They turned to see a man with a shaved head and piercing blue eyes, pointing a Glock 17 handgun at Nick's head.

Ruth recognised him as one of the men that had chased them from the offices of Global Escorts.

He waved the gun and snarled, 'Come with me.'

Without warning, Nick kicked out his right foot, plunging his heel into the armed man's hand and sending the Glock skidding along the deck.

The man came for him and threw a punch which cracked against Nick's temple. He winced but ran at the man, crashing his shoulder into him and knocking him into the bulwark which ran around the edge of the deck. He groaned and fell to the ground.

Ruth dashed across the deck and grabbed the Glock.

As the man tried to get up, Nick kicked him in the head and stood over him with his foot on his throat.

With the Glock now pointing at his face, Ruth looked down at him. 'Where are the women?'

The man smiled menacingly, his mouth and teeth now covered in blood. He raised his chin defiantly and shook his head.

'Where are the women?' Ruth repeated.

He smirked, and Nick kicked him even harder in the head.

His head rolled to one side – he was unconscious.

Ruth and Nick crept slowly across the deck towards the door from which they had seen the blonde man appear.

As she opened the door tentatively, Ruth could see metal steps leading down into the darkness of the lower deck. She wondered how many men were on the boat and if they were all armed.

Checking the Glock in her hand, she made sure that the safety mechanism was off.

Nick climbed cautiously down the steps first, with Ruth following. At the bottom, they crept silently towards the sound of music and laughter. It seemed as if someone was having a party.

A powerful arm shot over Ruth's shoulder, pulling back against her throat in a choke hold. She could hardly breathe.

'Drop the gun,' the blonde man demanded as she fought to get her breath.

'Okay, okay,' she gasped.

He looked at Nick. 'Stay back or I will break her neck.'

In a well-practised manoeuvre, Ruth threw her head back violently so that the back of her skull smashed against the blonde man's nose and face. At the same time, she stamped down as hard as she could onto the instep of his right foot.

He howled in pain, letting go of his choke hold.

Spinning around, she cracked the handle of the Glock against his temple with all her might and he crumpled to the floor in a heap.

Nick raised an eyebrow. 'Nice work.'

'Thanks,' Ruth croaked, feeling her throat. 'It's not the first time I've had to do that.'

As they continued to move through the lower deck, the music and laughter got louder.

They came to a large set of oak double doors. Ruth tried to open them but they were locked. There was a black security panel on the wall which clearly needed a code.

'Hello?' came a voice from the behind the door.

Ruth recognised it immediately.

'Sarah?'

'Ruth? Oh my God!' Sarah cried.

'Don't worry, we're going to get you out of there,' Ruth assured her. 'How many of you are there?'

'Six,' Sarah began to weep. 'I thought I was never going to see you again.'

'We'll be back to get you out, just stay calm.'

'Don't leave us here,' she pleaded.

As Ruth turned, two figures approached.

'You two should have stayed in your hotel.' It was Vernier and he was pointing a handgun at her face. A young man with a ponytail stood beside him but he appeared to be unarmed.

Ruth raised up the Glock and pointed it in Vernier's face. 'Yeah, but I wanted to stop perverted scumbags like you selling women to other perverted scumbags.'

A malevolent smile crossed Vernier's face. 'You're not going to shoot me, Detective. You're a British police officer. I'd be surprised if you'd ever held a gun before.'

Ruth put her finger on the trigger. 'Well I've got a big surprise for you then.'

In a sudden move, she pointed the gun at Vernier's shoulder and squeezed the trigger.

BANG!

The noise was deafening.

The gunshot sent Vernier reeling back against the wall as he dropped his gun.

Nick moved forward swiftly and grabbed the gun, pointing it at Vernier and the man with the ponytail.

'Jesus!' Vernier gasped as he clutched his blood-soaked shoulder. He couldn't believe she'd just shot him.

'Both of you get down on your knees!' Nick shouted.

They hesitated, and Ruth fired a warning shot above their heads.

'NOW!'

'You've just shot a senior French police officer,' Vernier groaned as he gripped his bleeding shoulder. 'You're going to prison. Both of you. Unless you leave now.'

Ruth ignored him and gestured to the security pad on the wall. 'What's the code to open these doors?'

Vernier looked at her with disdain. 'I'm not going to tell you that. And in about one minute this boat is going to be swarming with armed police officers. So, you two should go while you still have the chance.'

'GET BACK FROM THE DOOR LADIES!' Nick shouted to those inside.

With the gun in both hands, he fired three thunderous shots into the lock area and then gave the doors an almighty kick. They opened, and Ruth could see Sarah and five other woman huddled together by a huge circular bed.

Nick looked at Ruth. 'Problem solved.'

'Oh my God!' Ruth gasped as she looked at the women.

Emotion plugged her throat as her eyes met Sarah's.

Out of nowhere, Vernier scrambled past, grabbed Sarah from behind and put a knife to her throat.

At the same time, the man with the ponytail pulled out a handgun from the back of his jeans and fired at them.

Nick dived to the floor and shot the man in the stomach. He collapsed to the floor with a scream.

'Stay back or I'll kill her!' Vernier warned. The hand he was holding the knife with was trembling and dripping with blood.

'What are you going to do? Kill her, and then kill all these women and us?' Ruth said with steel in her tone. 'It's over. Put the knife down. You've done enough damage.'

Vernier shook his head. 'No. I don't care anymore. I don't care what damage I do.'

Ruth took aim with the Glock and pointed it at his forehead. 'Drop the knife, now!' she thundered.

'No, no,' Vernier stammered with a smirk. 'You may have the guts to shoot my shoulder but you do not have it in you to kill a man. So, both of you need to leave right now or I will slit her throat.'

Ruth looked at Sarah's terrified face. She had been through so much. Ruth wasn't leaving without her. Giving Sarah an imperceptible look, she just hoped Sarah would read her intentions.

Lowering the Glock to her side, Ruth looked at Vernier and nodded. 'Okay. Then we have to go.'

Nick glared at her uncertainly. 'What are you talking about?'

'I'm not taking the risk of him killing Sarah. Nothing is worth that.'

Nick was horrified as he gestured to Sarah and the women who were still cowering on the bed. 'We can't just leave them all here.'

'We have no choice.'

As she turned, she spotted out of the corner of her eye that Vernier had ever so slightly relaxed his grip on Sarah.

'I can't believe you're doing this,' Nick whispered. 'Are you really going to walk out of here without Sarah.'

'No, of course I'm not!'

In that split second, Ruth made her move.

Sarah must have sensed what Ruth was doing because she pushed the knife away from her throat and shoved Vernier backwards.

Ruth raised the Glock and took aim.

Vernier stumbled and looked at her with widened eyes.

BANG! BANG!

Ruth shot him between the eyes and then in the chest.

He was dead before he hit the floor.

Nick flinched. 'Bloody hell, Ruth!'

Sarah ran into Ruth's arms and wept.

'If you ever disappear again, I will bloody kill you, understand?' Ruth cried through her tears as they hugged.

CHAPTER 24

It was gone midnight, and Ruth sat drinking coffee in the main meeting room at the DGSE building. Nick was next to her signing his preliminary statement about the events of the evening. The lights of Paris glimmered as she glanced out of the window, and the night air seemed to be filled with the incessant sound of sirens. She was secure in the knowledge that Sarah and the other women were being held at a secret location by armed DGSE agents.

The last hour had been a whirlwind as agents in the DGSE, the Paris Police, and the French government began to hear about what had happened aboard the *Celestine* less than two hours earlier. The French president and British prime minister were being kept informed of developments, as was the French cabinet. There had been a total media blackout, although major news sources such as Fox, CNN and the BBC were reporting that there had been gunshots heard and a lot of police activity surrounding a vessel on the Seine. No one had yet linked the ownership of the *Celestine* to Patrice Le Bon, but Ruth knew that it was only a matter of time.

The door opened and Camille Moreau walked in, holding more folders and paperwork. She was followed by a man in his 60s, with silver hair and a chiselled jawline.

'Ruth and Nick, this is Jean Regas, Director of the DGSE. Jean, this is DI Hunter and DS Evans of the British police.'

'It is good to meet you,' he muttered as he took off his jacket, hung it over a chair and sat down. 'You have had quite a night I hear?'

'Yes.' Ruth gave an ironic laugh. 'Quite a night doesn't even begin to do it justice.'

'And we have one dead police captain, with three other officers in hospital, one of whom is critical,' he informed them. 'I think you have a right to know that the DGSE has been running an investigation into Capitaine Vernier and his links to organised crime for several years. Tonight, we arrested a further twelve police officers in Paris who worked with him. I want to assure you that he, and the other officers on the boat, were evil, corrupt men.'

Ruth nodded in agreement. She had no idea what the repercussions would be in the UK of off-duty police officers using firearms. It wasn't something that she wanted to give too much thought to right now.

Moreau indicated the printout in front of her. 'We're arranging for all the women who were on the boat to be transported home safely. At the moment, we're trying to locate their families.'

'Sarah will be coming with me, naturally,' Ruth said.

Moreau smiled. 'Yes, of course, if that's what she wants.'

'She does. And I want us to travel by train. The Eurostar to St Pancras. I'm assuming that anyone wanting to stop her from leaving will be expecting us to fly.'

'That seems sensible,' Regas agreed. 'You will all travel under false names on the passenger list, and we will assign you an armed DGSE agent who will accompany you to London. I understand that you have an Interpol liaison officer?'

'Oliver Trelford,' Ruth said.

Regas looked at Moreau. 'Do we know him?'

'Relatively new,' she replied. 'He's taken over from Ian Harrison for the foreseeable future.'

Regas ran his hand through his hair as he looked over at them. 'It might be that he wishes to accompany you on your journey to make sure that everything runs smoothly.'

Moreau's phone rang and she took the call.

'Not a problem,' Ruth said. 'It was Oliver's tip-off that confirmed the boat's name was *Celestine*.'

'Okay. That is settled then. I probably don't need to tell you this as you are experienced police officers, but I would advise against talking to any section of the media.'

'I have no intention of talking to anyone about what happened tonight unless I'm forced to,' Ruth clarified.

Regas sat forward on his chair. 'That's good to hear.'

Moreau ended her phone call. 'Sarah will be taken to your hotel in one hour, and an armed agent will be stationed outside your door all night.'

Ruth sighed heavily. 'Thank you.'

Back in her hotel room, Ruth came out of the bathroom and gazed at the woman she'd fallen in love with all those years ago. Sarah was wearing a white towelling hotel robe and laying on the bed, propped up by pillows.

'I've run you a bath,' Ruth told her, 'and it's the temperature of lava, as you like it, ma'am.'

'Isn't it *drawn*?'

Ruth took her time before replying. 'Isn't *what* drawn?'

'If you're very posh,' Sarah said in a cut-glass accent, 'someone draws a bath for you. The butler comes and says "I've drawn a bath for you, my lady."'

'Bloody hell,' Ruth laughed. 'Get you.'

She went towards her and held out her hand. Sarah smiled as she took it, but Ruth could feel her trembling.

'Sorry,' Sarah apologised as she eased herself off the bed. 'You're really shaky.'

Sarah tried to steady herself. 'It's the heroin withdrawal.'

'I thought you were taking methadone?'

'It's not the same, and the dose is lower. I've got some diazepam but I'm still going to get withdrawal symptoms. It's horrible. I've come off heroin a couple of times in the last few years, but the withdrawal symptoms are so harrowing that people start taking it again. It's a vicious cycle.'

Ruth gave a long sigh. 'So much has happened to both of us in the past seven years, but I never thought I was going to hear you say "I've come off heroin a couple of times ..."'

Once Ruth had helped her into the bathroom, Sarah slipped off her robe and she climbed into the bath. Ruth looked at her naked body. She was skinnier and paler than she'd ever seen her, but that wasn't surprising. There were two deep scars on either side of her stomach.'

Sarah leant back and closed her eyes. 'God that feels good.'

Resting her head on the back of the bath, she blinked open her eyes and rubbed her face.

'How did you get those scars?' Ruth asked after a few seconds.

'This one on the left was a Polish man who just decided that he was going to stab me for no reason.'

'When you say a Polish man do you mean ...?'

'What ... a punter? Yes.' She said the words lightly, but her attitude made it clear she was feeling some anger.

'Sorry,' Ruth mumbled. 'I'm just trying to get my head around so much.'

'Bully for you,' Sarah snapped.

There was an awkward silence.

Ruth looked at her.

'What?' Sarah challenged as she whipped her head towards her.

'Nothing.' Ruth knew that anything she said right now was going to be taken as inflammatory.

'Imagine experiencing things like that and having it in your head all day, every single day!'

'I'm sorry.' Ruth tried to force an empathetic smile. 'It's okay. I'll ... I'll leave you to have a bath and I'll look at the room service menu.'

Sarah glanced at Ruth uncomfortably. 'I'm damaged goods, you do understand that?'

Ruth saw the wounded look in Sarah's eyes. 'No, you're not,' she said, speaking softly. 'It's nothing we can't get past eventually.'

'Don't be so fucking naïve, Ruth. This ...' she said, tapping her head, '... this is totally broken. Damaged beyond any repair. I'm not the same person.'

'Don't say that!'

'I've spent seven years worrying that at any moment I could be murdered. I've been forced to sleep with countless vile, disgusting men,' Sarah said, becoming loud and animated. 'I've been stabbed and beaten, and I'm addicted to heroin. I don't think I deserved any of that.'

'You didn't!'

She looked quickly at Ruth before continuing. 'But it happened, and I'm the one who has to deal with it, not you. You need to understand that you don't come back from any of that intact. I can't be repaired. Talking to a therapist isn't going to help, and taking some bloody anti-depressants isn't going to cure me of all that fucked up trauma!'

'I'm a police officer,' Ruth said gently. 'I do understand trauma.'

Ruth reached out her hand to stroke her face but Sarah knocked it away.

'No, no you don't,' Sarah said accusingly. 'You see its effects. You see the pain and misery it causes and you try to pick up the pieces. But you don't understand what it feels like.'

Ruth felt her patience waver. 'You haven't got a monopoly on feeling terrible pain and anxiety over the last seven years,' she cut in sharply. 'You got on a bloody train and vanished. I thought you'd been abducted and murdered, but I also had the hope that you were still out there somewhere. Do you know what that feels like Sarah? It's that endless, gnawing hope that's the real killer. It got to the point where I'd work on a murder case and envy the family because they had a body to bury. Their son or daughter, their father or mother. They had the gift of certainty. They got to say goodbye, draw a line under their grief and try to move forward, however difficult that was.'

A few seconds of tense silence passed.

Sarah lifted up her shaking hand and stared at it as the bath water dripped onto her leg.

'We're just not the same people any more, are we?' she whispered, tears streaming down her face.

'No,' Ruth agreed quietly. 'I don't think we can be.'

'So, what does that mean for us?'

Ruth looked at her. 'I just don't know.'

CHAPTER 25

Ruth sat looking out at the Gare du Nord platform from their Eurostar train. She was sitting opposite Sarah, but somehow felt the need to avoid eye contact. The DGSE had arranged for them to travel in an empty section of a Business Premier carriage for security reasons. A DGSE agent sat at the far end of the carriage beside the door. Ruth knew that somewhere under his suit he was carrying a gun, which was a relief after the events of the past few days.

Nick checked his watch and then pointed to a café on the platform. 'I'm just going to pop out there to get a brew. Anyone want anything?'

'A brew?' Sarah laughed. 'I haven't heard anyone call tea *a brew* in donkey's years. Yeah, I'd love a brew, Nick.'

He grinned. 'Coming up. Ruth?'

'Take a guess.'

'Flat white, then,' he said without hesitation as he went to the far end of the carriage.

'God, you two really do know each other very well,' Sarah remarked gesturing to Nick as he left.

Ruth smiled. 'We're like an old married couple.'

'Must be nice to work with someone like that?'

'Yeah, it really is.'

Since their heated and emotional conversation the night before, Ruth and Sarah had said very little of great meaning to each other. They had held each other as they slept together on top of the duvet of the hotel bed. But since then, their conversation had been limited to superficial pleasantries.

'Are we okay?' Ruth asked after a few seconds of slightly awkward silence. She didn't really know what that meant, but she wanted to clear the air a little before the journey started.

Sarah picked at a thread on her sleeve. 'We're okay now, I guess. Are we *going to be* okay? I've no idea.'

'It's all right, I didn't want a long discussion. I just wanted to clear the air a bit.'

'Yeah, so did I.' Sarah smiled, then looked past Ruth and raised her brow in a show of surprise. 'Looks like we've got a visitor.'

Ruth spun nervously but to her relief she saw that it was just Oliver Trelford, who gave her one of his trademark awkward waves as he showed the DGSE agent his identification.

'It's Oliver,' Ruth said with relief. 'He's from Interpol. Nice guy despite geeky first appearances.'

'Sorry, sorry,' he apologised as he reached them. He took off his coat and put his laptop case down on the table across from them. He had a few English newspapers with him. 'I think you've grown accustomed to my timekeeping, haven't you Ruth?'

'It's part of your charm, Oliver,' she quipped.

'Oh God, is it?' Trelford laughed a little too loud and then sat himself down at his table. 'Third time I've done one of these official Interpol escorts back to London.'

'Are you coming straight back here?' Ruth asked.

'God, no. I'm definitely having a night out in London. A friend is taking me to a new play in Haymarket, then dinner at The Ivy, so I'm looking forward to that.'

'Sounds good,' Sarah said with a smile.

As Trelford took his laptop out of his bag, he gestured to it and asked, 'At the risk of being a bit of an old spoilsport, I've got a mountain of work. Do you mind if I just crack on with this?'

Ruth laughed. 'Don't worry, we're not going to be offended.'

'And we're probably too tired to be decent company,' Sarah added.

Nick arrived back with the teas and Ruth's flat white.

'Thanks Nick. Here's to a decent brew,' Sarah laughed, picking up her tea.

'Yeah, well we're in France so I wouldn't get your hopes up.' Nick chuckled at his own witticism.

They all laughed.

Ruth took a long sip of her coffee, which was perfect. There were the sounds of a whistle, the doors closing, and then an announcement over the train's onboard PA system telling them they were about to depart.

There was a poignant silence in the carriage as the train set into motion and pulled very slowly out of Gare du Nord.

'We'll always have Paris,' Ruth whispered to herself.

'Humphrey Bogart?' Sarah asked.

'The best final line of a movie ever,' Ruth said. She then closed her eyes and rested her head back against the seat. She listened to the comforting rhythmical sound of the wheels below, propelling them northwards from Paris and towards home.

'Ruth says you have a daughter?' Sarah asked after a while.

'Megan,' Nick replied.

'And you really asked her to be Megan's godmother?' Sarah laughed, pointing to Ruth.

Ruth's eyes remained closed. 'Just because I have my eyes closed, doesn't mean I can't hear you Sarah!'

They all grinned.

'You'll be glad to get back to her, won't you?' Sarah asked. 'And it's Amanda, isn't it?'

'Yeah, I can't wait to see them both,' Nick admitted.

'Ruth tells me you're having a winter wedding. How wonderfully romantic of you. How did you propose? Was that very romantic too?'

Ruth opened her eyes and raised an eyebrow at Nick. 'Romantic? Jesus!'

'Hey!' Nick protested. 'It was very romantic.'

'You used a rusty old metal detector, Nick!' Ruth laughed.

'What?' Sarah exclaimed with a smile. 'How do you propose with a rusty old metal detector?'

'Okay, bear with me. I'd buried the ring. I got Amanda to have a try with the metal detector in the garden and then, hey presto, she found the buried ring.'

'Aww, that's actually pretty cute.'

'Scrabbling around in the mud in Nick's back garden isn't cute,' Ruth corrected.

'Well it was very romantic in my head,' Nick said. 'Less so in reality as she was heavily pregnant and very reluctant to use the metal detector ... You'll have to come to the wedding.'

'Erm ... yes,' Sarah replied hesitantly after an awkward few seconds.

'Sorry,' he apologised. 'I ... I wasn't making any presumptions.'

'No no, it's fine,' Ruth reassured him and then looked over at Sarah, 'but I *am* going to need a plus-one in a few months' time.'

Nick sipped his tea. 'Sorry if I've made things a bit awkward. Shall we talk about something else?'

Sarah smiled. 'It's fine. Really. I would love to come to your wedding. If I'm honest, Ruth and I haven't got past what we're doing today and maybe tomorrow.'

'I completely understand,' Nick laughed and then gestured to the end of the carriage. 'Maybe I should just go and hide in the toilet for a bit.'

Sarah grabbed her bag, delved inside and pulled out an eight-inch golden statue of the Eiffel Tower. 'Look what I bought when we arrived at the station.'

Ruth looked at it as if she had a bad taste in her mouth. 'Dear God, it's disgusting!'

Nick laughed. 'Very tasteful.'

'I like it.' Sarah picked it up. 'It's bloody heavy. It's made of metal.'

Ruth moved the statue to the centre of the table beside the window. 'There you go. Pride of place for the rest of the journey.' She then looked from Sarah to Nick. 'You know what, I think I'm going to close my eyes and have a nap for a bit.'

'Sounds like a good plan,' Sarah agreed.

Nick pulled out his AirPods. 'I'll put these on to drown out the snoring.'

Ruth gave him a smile tinged with sarcasm. She closed her eyes and felt herself drifting away almost immediately.

By the time Ruth woke, the sun had risen high into the sky. Its rays, filtered by the railside trees, streamed through the window, mottling the carriage with irregular shapes of light. Sarah sat across from her, fast asleep. Her legs were curled up under her and she was breathing softly. She looked so cute and vulnerable.

Nick was listening to something on his AirPods and grinning like a naughty schoolboy.

Trelford, who was busily thumbing through his newspapers, stopped for a second and looked over at her.

'Was I asleep for long?' Ruth asked with a yawn.

'Only half an hour or so,' he replied with a kind smile.

Ruth stretched out her back which was still sore and bruised from where she had been shot.

Trelford sat forward and held up the front of *The Sun* newspaper. It featured a photograph of a female actress at an awards ceremony receiving her golden BAFTA from Lord David Weaver. 'I'm guessing when all this comes out, Lord Weaver won't be needing his designer dinner suit anymore.'

'No, he definitely won't,' she agreed.

Nick took out his AirPods. 'Just finished a Peter Crouch podcast series. It's hilarious. In the final episode, Prince William tells them a story about how he used to carry around one of those toy laser pens. He'd secretly shine the red dot on one of his friends and tell them it was the laser sights from one of his close protection officer's sniper rifles.'

Ruth giggled. It was a funny story.

'How long before we get into the tunnel?' Nick asked.

Trelford looked at his watch. 'Twenty minutes or so.'

Ruth pouted. 'I'm not a fan of tunnels. I get a bit claustrophobic.'

'Don't worry,' Trelford assured her, 'it's nothing like the London Underground.'

'Just to check, the witness protection officers are meeting us off the train at St Pancras?' she queried.

'That's right, plus two agents from MI5,' Trelford confirmed as he looked at his phone. 'Anyone else struggling to use the WiFi in here?'

Nick shook his head. 'Not me.'

Trelford got up from his seat and gestured to the door at the far end. 'I'm going to try out there for a second. I need to confirm my hotel for tonight.'

As Trelford left, Nick stood up and stretched his legs. 'Nice guy, Oliver, isn't he? I wouldn't mind working at Interpol.'

Ruth arched her brows. 'Oh yes, and how are your languages?'

'My Welsh is pretty good, ta. Otherwise pretty woeful, if I'm honest.'

As Nick strolled down the carriage and looked out of the window, Ruth grabbed the copy of *The Sun* from Trelford's table.

'You seen this?' she asked, raising the front page so Nick could see.

'Yeah. I've always thought Weaver was a prick after he did that TV show.'

Ruth peered at the photo of Lord Weaver grinning as he stood next to the glamorous British actress.

You've got a nasty surprise coming, you murdering bastard, he thought.

And then something struck her.

'Shit!' Ruth cried out loud. Her pulse started to race. Something was wrong.

'You okay?' Nick asked as he wandered back up the carriage towards her.

She gestured to the photo on the front of *The Sun.* 'Oliver just showed me this photo and said *Lord Weaver won't be needing his designer dinner suit anymore.*'

'So? If Sarah testifies, he'll go to jail for murder.'

'How does Oliver know that Sarah saw Lord Weaver kill that girl seven years ago?' Ruth asked with a growing sense of unease. 'I didn't tell him.'

'Who else did you talk to in Paris?'

'I told Camille Moreau that it was a peer of the British realm, but I made a conscious effort not to use his name. So, how does Oliver know that? Seriously?'

'You seem spooked ...'

'I *am* bloody spooked, Nick! There are eight people on the planet that know exactly what happened in that hotel room in 2013. Weaver and the other four men who helped him cover it up. Sarah, who witnessed it. And me and you. That's it.'

Ruth reached across the table and tapped Sarah's arm, trying to rouse her. 'Sarah? Sarah?'

She opened an eye and squinted. 'What's going on?'

'Listen to me. Did you tell Oliver Trelford about what you saw in the hotel in 2013?'

'What? No, of course not. I've hardly spoken to him.'

'You didn't mention any names?'

'No. What's going on?' she groaned as she sat up in her seat

Nick pointed to the end of their carriage. 'Not to add to the general sense of panic, but our DGSE agent has gone. I noticed that he wasn't there about ten minutes ago and he still isn't back.'

'Shit!' Ruth's head began to race.

'You think that Oliver Trelford is the leak?' Nick asked.

'He has to be. We told him about Ancille and Gus. And now they're both dead.'

Sarah's face was clouded with confusion. 'I'm completely lost,' she said.

'Nick! Stay here with Sarah!'

'Where the hell are you going?'

'Just stay here!'

Ruth made her way to the door at the end of the carriage. The seat where the DGSE agent had been sitting was empty and there was nothing to suggest that he had ever been there.

The automatic door slid open and she moved slowly forwards, scanning left and right as she went.

Where the hell is Trelford? He's disappeared.

Her pulse was racing and her mouth was dry. If Trelford was the leak, then Le Bon, Saratov and Golkin knew that Sarah was on the train heading for the UK. And maybe they would try to stop her getting there.

Where was Trelford? And where was their DGSE agent?

She came to the curved automatic door to the toilet. Glancing both ways, she hit the green 'open' button. There was a *hiss* and the door moved back slowly.

A man was sitting on the toilet.

It was the DGSE agent.

Ruth stepped back quickly. 'Oh, I'm so sorry,' she sput-tered, 'I didn't know anyone was in here.'

The agent didn't react or even turn to look at her.

'Hello?'

Ruth's stomach lurched as she moved forward into the large space and looked at the agent.

There was a neat bullet hole in the centre of his forehead, and an explosion of brain matter on the wall behind him.

His darkened, dead eyes just stared at her.

Oh my God!

For a moment, she thought she was going to be sick.

Get it together, Ruth, she thought to herself.

There was no doubt now that there was something serious-ly wrong and that they were in extreme danger.

She looked at the door, which had now automatically closed, and then had a thought.

Moving closer to the agent, she reached inside his jacket and felt around both sides for a gun.

Nothing.

I thought he was supposed to be armed?

As she turned to go back to the door, she caught sight of something on the agent's calf where his trousers were crumpled around his ankles.

It was a leather strap.

Patting down the trouser leg, she saw the strap was at-tached to a leather ankle holster holding a SIG Pro automatic handgun.

That's where he kept it.

She took the gun from the holster and studied it. She had only ever fired Glocks. The SIG Pro couldn't be that different, could it? She placed it in the waistband at the back of her trousers and closed her jacket.

As she came out of the toilet, she dropped to a crouch and crept back towards their carriage.

What the hell is going on? Has Trelford killed the agent or is there someone else on the train?

She was just a few feet from the door into their carriage, keeping low. With a quick glance, she looked inside to see what was going on. Nick and Sarah were sitting at the table talking, and Trelford was back at his seat, typing on his laptop.

She pushed the button and the door slid open.

'Our DGSE agent has been murdered!' she exclaimed. 'We need to get off the train!'

She glared at the back of Trelford's head, waiting for him to turn around.

Nick and Sarah didn't react and said nothing.

Something wasn't right.

She felt the cold metal of a gun barrel push hard into her temple.

Someone had been standing inside the carriage at the side of the door.

Shit!

'I think you should come and sit down,' said a man's voice with a Russian accent.

She turned to look.

It was Golkin.

His face and hair were strangely colourless and his eyes grey and slightly bloodshot.

Keeping his gun pressed to her head, he forced her to walk back to her seat.

'Sit there,' he commanded quietly.

Ruth sat down and glared at Trelford whose face remained unchanged. 'Why?' she asked.

Trelford looked at her, a tight smile on his lips. 'Why do you think? Can you imagine the pittance I get paid to work for Interpol?'

Nick's face tightened. 'Money? Jesus! What about the people who get killed or hurt because you're feeding information to scumbags like him?'

Golkin smiled, revealing crooked and yellow teeth. 'Most of them deserve it. Collateral damage.'

'Tell that to the widow of an innocent bar owner who is now lying in the mortuary,' Ruth said forcibly.

Nick's eyes searched Trelford's face. 'You tipped us off about the Celestine. That doesn't make any sense.'

'Capitaine Vernier and his men were meant to capture you when you boarded the boat. And then I guess you would have been found floating in some French river a few days later.'

Golkin glanced at his watch. He took a six-inch silencer from his pocket and began to screw it to the end of his Glock 19M.

'What now?' Ruth asked, as dread trickled down her spine.

'Mr Golkin and I are going to be leaving the train,' Trelford replied.

'And you're taking Sarah with you?'

'God no,' he laughed. 'She's far too much of a liability to be left alive. And so are you two, I'm afraid.'

Golkin raised his gun and pointed it directly at Ruth's head. The black hole of the barrel seemed to be in line with her eyes. Terror coursed through her veins.

This is it. This is the moment that I die.

She turned her head slightly and locked eyes with Sarah who cried out, 'No!'

'Be quiet!' Golkin roared.

Ruth closed her eyes and prepared to be shot.

She flinched and held her breath.

She heard a thud, like a hammer against thick wood.

Nothing.

She realised that she was still very much alive, and opened her eyes.

What the ...?

Across from her, Trelford was slumped over the table. A pool of blood began to form around his head, then dripped slowly down onto the carpet.

Golkin then aimed his gun at Sarah. 'Sorry.'

Ruth sat forward slowly. She pulled the SIG Pro from behind her, swung it towards Golkin, and fired.

CRACK!

The bullet hit him in the chest.

As he staggered backwards, he fired his gun. The bullet hit the carriage window, smashing it into a cascade of broken glass.

The carriage was suddenly like a thunderous wind tunnel. Papers, cups, and objects swirled around in the air.

Nick sprang forward and grabbed Golkin's wrist, trying to wrestle the gun from his hand.

Another bullet was fired and thudded into one of the seats.

Gripping the SIG Pro, Ruth just couldn't get a clean shot – Nick was in the way.

Golkin punched Nick square in the face and sent him flying.

Ruth then had a side view of Golkin and fired, but missed. Jesus!

Golkin held his gun with both hands, turned, and fired a shot at Ruth.

She instinctively ducked, and the bullet missed her and hammered into the wall behind.

Then, Sarah lunged across the table, pulling at Golkin's long hair and clawing at his face. With a mighty shove, he tossed her away and she was thrown backwards.

Ruth fired again. The bullet hit Golkin's upper arm. He winced but then turned and fired at her again.

Ruth felt as if someone had stamped on her hand as the SIG Pro went flying. There was an intense burning sensation. As she looked down, she saw that the bullet had pierced the flesh on her right hand.

Standing up, she faced Golkin.

'Do it!' she yelled at him. 'Just do it!'

This time there wasn't going to be an escape.

He raised the Glock level with her eyeline.

She stared down the black barrel and waited for the end.

Suddenly, there was a blood-curdling scream.

Out of the corner of her eye, she spotted Sarah launching herself through mid-air. In her hand, she had the statue of the Eiffel Tower.

She knocked Golkin off balance and tackled him to the ground. She sat astride him and drove the tip of the statue into his throat.

Golkin gripped the statue as blood trickled from the corners of his mouth and gushed from his neck. He gasped for air as he writhed on the floor.

And then he stopped moving.

He was dead.

Trembling violently, Sarah got up slowly. Her shirt clung to her, glued by the blood that had fountained from Golkin's wound.

'I j-j-just want t-t-to go home,' she stuttered through chattering teeth. She wept as she turned to Ruth.

Ruth put her arms around her. 'I know you do. So do I.'

CHAPTER 26

48 hours later

It was late morning, and Ruth and Sarah had decided to head up to the rooftop restaurant at their hotel in Russell Square in the centre of London. Until further notice, they were confined to the hotel except for essential journeys when they would be accompanied by an MI5 Close Protection Officer. Nick had left early that morning to return home to Llancastell.

The past two days had been an endless series of meetings, debriefings, medicals, and long hours spent in their hotel room. Events on their Eurostar train were still being referred to on the news as 'an incident involving a firearm'. There had been some media speculation that the incident was somehow linked with the events on the Seine.

Ruth and Nick had met with the Home Secretary and the Commissioner of the Metropolitan Police to discuss their involvement in the two very serious incidents. It wasn't clear at this stage whether they would face disciplinary charges. However, the Commissioner had made it clear that she believed Ruth and Nick had shown the utmost bravery and fortitude in bringing a horrendous sex trafficking ring to justice. It seemed that it was only a matter of time before the men leading the ring would be arrested.

Sarah had been convinced to turn evidence against Lord David Weaver, Jamie Parsons, Jurgen Kessler, Sergei Saratov and Patrice Le Bon. She would go on record and testify to witnessing the murder of Gabriela Cardoso, the seventeen-year-old au pair from Portugal who she had now identified from photographs. Until a trial, Sarah would have to enter the Witness Protection Programme with a new identity. In return for her testimony, she would face no criminal charges and would be able to choose a location to start a new life.

The rooftop restaurant and bar were spectacular, and incredibly chic and luxurious. Ruth gestured to a table that had magnificent views to the south-east of London's Square Mile, St Paul's, The Shard and Canary Wharf.

As they settled themselves at the table, a waiter approached.

'Can I get you some drinks?' he asked.

Sarah looked at Ruth. 'White wine?'

Ruth nodded in confirmation. 'White wine.'

'Of course, I will bring you the wine list.'

Sarah put on a pair of sunglasses that were very 70s Boho.

'They really suit you,' Ruth said. 'You look like that British actress from the 60s or 70s.'

Sarah laughed. 'Well that doesn't narrow it down.'

'She was in *Bullitt* with Steve McQueen and also *The Deep*. You know?'

Sarah tapped her lips in a show of contemplation. 'Oh I do know actually. Jacqueline Bisset, wasn't it?'

'Correct.'

Ruth's phone buzzed and she saw a missed call from DCI Drake.

'Anything important?' Sarah asked, gesturing to the phone.

'Work. I think my DCI wants to know if and when I can come back.'

'And what do you think?'

'How do you mean?'

'Will you go back to being a copper in North Wales?'

The waiter arrived, handed them both a wine list, and then poured some water in each of their glasses.

'Of course!' Ruth said. 'That's my life.'

Sarah glanced at her quickly, as if she'd been expecting a different answer. 'Oh, okay. I just wasn't sure.'

'That doesn't mean you can't be in my life though, does it?'

'I don't know. I never imagined myself living outside of London.'

'I would have thought North Wales would be perfect for you after all you've been through? It's so peaceful.'

Sarah picked up her water. The glass hovered in front of her lips but she didn't drink from it. 'When I spent all those years away, I imagined what life would be like if I ever got away. If I ever got home. I wanted to swim in Brockwell Lido on a summer's day. Sit in a pub overlooking the Thames. Go to some incredible gay club and leave at dawn.'

Ruth looked at her uncertainly.

'I don't understand what you're saying,' she said.

'A village in North Wales? What the hell would I do?'

'You'd be with me.'

The waiter arrived back at their table. 'Have you managed to have a look at the wine list?'

Sarah turned her gaze to him. 'A bottle of Sancerre, if you've got it?'

'A bottle of Sancerre. Of course, madame.'

The waiter left them and Ruth gave her a quizzical look 'You know about wine?'

'I spent a lot of time in the company of very rich men. I got to know about wine, along with many other things.'

'It sounds like being in North Wales with me isn't going to be enough?' Ruth asked, failing to hide the hurt she felt.

'You know the best thing about London?' Sarah asked.

Ruth shook her head.

'You can hide yourself away when you want to. You can make yourself anonymous. And then when you want to go out, be with other people, you get to choose that. I get the feeling that where you live, everyone would know your business.'

'You're in witness protection. You might not be able to stay in London.'

'I've already asked them. Even if it's a suburb, it's something that could be arranged.'

'I didn't know that,' Ruth said dejectedly.

'I'm sorry. I didn't want to tell you until we'd had *this* conversation.'

The waiter arrived back, showed Sarah the bottle, and then opened it before pouring two glasses of wine.

As he left them, Ruth picked up the glass and took a sip. 'You really do know wine.'

'It's nice isn't it?'

They looked at each other over the table as they sipped their drinks.

Sarah pushed her sunglasses up onto her hair. 'Ruth, I don't know what I'm doing. I don't know what I want. My head is a mess.'

'Isn't that a good reason not to be on your own?'

'I'm not sure. I think being on my own might be just what I need. I don't want to have to compromise on anything. I don't want to have to negotiate the ups and downs of a relationship. I just want to try and get *me* back.'

'What about love?' Ruth asked.

'Overrated.'

Ruth felt tears well in her eyes. 'Overrated? Okay.'

Sarah pursed her lips together. 'Sorry. That wasn't very kind.'

'You've been through an unimaginable hell in the past few years Sarah. I can't begin to understand how you feel or what that's done to you. But I always imagined that if I ever found you, we would find a way to be together. I guess that makes me naïve.'

Sarah shook her head. 'Romantic, not naïve. I get the feeling that in those years that you searched for me, your memories of what we had became ... a little rose-tinted.'

Ruth blinked away a tear. 'You were the love of my life Sarah!'

'And you were mine ... but it was such a long, long time ago.'

'We were happy, weren't we?'

'Were we?'

'I don't understand,' Ruth said.

Sarah sighed. 'I had an affair, Ruth. I didn't have an affair because I was too happy.'

Ruth wiped her face with the linen napkin. She felt crushed by what Sarah was telling her.

'So, what happens now?' Ruth asked. 'We just don't see each other? We just get on with our lives?'

'I don't know.' Sarah shook her head wearily. 'I'm just trying to get through today without losing my mind completely.

And then tomorrow, I'll do the same. I can't factor in you or us or anyone.'

Ruth stared at her, mute and uncomprehending. She took a deep breath as more tears came. 'I didn't see this coming,' she said finally.

'I'm sorry.'

'I feel like such an idiot.'

Sarah reached over and took Ruth's hand. 'I just need a lot of time to find me again, and to work out what I want my life to become.'

'I understand that. I just thought I would be part of that journey, helping you on the way.'

'I'm sorry,' Sarah said. 'I have to do this for myself.'

CHAPTER 27

Ruth opened her front door, stepped inside, and revelled in the reassuring smell of home. She wheeled in her suitcase and noticed the television was on.

'Mum?'

It was Ella.

Ruth smiled. 'Hey! You didn't tell me that you were going to break into my house to surprise me!'

Ella walked over and gave her a tight hug. 'Ha, ha. You gave me a set of keys, remember.'

As Ruth took off her coat, Ella pointed down the hallway.

'Aren't you forgetting someone?' she asked with a beaming smile. 'Where is she?'

'She's not here.'

'Very funny,' Ella said as she walked towards the door.

'Seriously. She hasn't come back with me.'

'What? I don't understand.'

'Sarah's not coming back here.'

'Eh?'

'She wants to stay in London.'

Ella's eyes widened. 'That's ridiculous!'

'I sort of understand where she's coming from,' Ruth said unsurely.

'Bloody hell, Mum. You spent seven years looking for her. It nearly killed you. You grieved for her all that time, and now she's decided that she doesn't want to be with you?'

Ruth blinked as tears welled in her eyes. 'I can't make her want to be with me, can I?'

'That's so fucked up!' Ella snapped as she went over and hugged her mother tightly. 'I'm so sorry.'

'It's going to be fine,' Ruth muttered under her breath, 'I just need to get drunk.'

Ella led her by the hand into the kitchen, and poured a large glass of Rioja from the bottle that she had already opened.

'Here you go.'

'Thanks,' Ruth said, looking and feeling utterly lost.

Ella furrowed her brow. 'I just thought that if you ever found Sarah, you would be together.'

'So did I,' Ruth sighed. 'But you've got to remember what she's been through in the past seven years. And there's more stuff that I haven't even begun to tell you about. It was naïve of me to think that we could just go back to living together after everything that's happened.'

'I think you try to work through stuff,' Ella huffed.

Ruth took a long swig of wine. She just wanted to switch off.

Ella reached out and took her hand. 'I thought you loved each other?'

'So did I, darling. So did I.'

Spinning Megan around in his arms, Nick grinned.

'Daddy, daddy!' she yelled.

'Put her down,' Amanda laughed, 'or she'll be sick in your face.'

Nick put Megan down on the sofa. 'Here you go, my little princess.'

After the past few days, he couldn't imagine that he would ever want to be anywhere else but where he was standing right now.

Amanda came over, put her arms around him, and they kissed.

He looked into her big brown eyes and melted. 'God, I've missed you so much.'

Amanda gave him a mischievous smirk. 'What's got into you? Not like you to be all gooey. I'm not sure I like it.'

Nick laughed. 'Oh thanks, I can't win, can I?'

'And I assume that you've forgotten that you've hidden a big bottle of French perfume somewhere in your case that you're going to give to me later?'

'I'm definitely going to give it to you later, but there's no perfume I'm afraid,' he said with a twinkle in his eye.

She pushed his arm playfully. 'You were in bloody Paris, you loser!'

Nick slumped down into a soft armchair and pulled Amanda down onto his lap. Megan looked over, giggled, and went back to watching CBeebies.

He raised an eyebrow as he looked at her. 'Trust me, it wasn't that kind of trip.'

She studied his face. 'You've got a bit of a black eye. What the hell have you been doing?'

He gave her an ironic smile. 'Yeah, well you should see the other guy!'

He wasn't about to tell her that the 'other guy' was a Russian assassin who'd had a statue of the Eiffel Tower thrust into his throat and died in front of him in a bloody, gurgling mess.

'I assume Sarah is coming back here to live with Ruth?' Amanda asked.

'To be fair, we didn't talk about it. I guess they'll sort that out.'

Amanda pointed to the television. 'There was a thing on the news the other night about a police operation on the Seine and gunshots?'

'Hey, I'm not saying anything.'

Alarm sounded in Amanda's voice. 'Oh my God. Was that anything to do with you and Ruth?'

'I think I would be breaking the Official Secrets Act if I tell you anything about it.'

'Bloody hell, Nick! Well when you're galivanting around pretending that you're bloody James Bond, can you remember that you have two beautiful girls in your life that you're responsible for,' she said scornfully.

'Sorry, you've lost me. Two beautiful girls? There's one sitting on the sofa watching the telly, but the other one ...'

Amanda took his face with both hands. 'DS Nick Evans, that's not even funny.'

Then she kissed him hard on the mouth.

CHAPTER 28
24 hours later

Ruth sat watching the BBC News. Ella came in with a glass of wine, handed it to her, and sat down.

'Thanks, darling. Are you not having one?'

'I'm going to drive home in bit, if that's okay?'

Ruth smiled. 'Of course. You don't have to ask if it's okay.'

'Are you going to be all right here on your own?' Ella asked.

Ruth rolled her eyes and picked up her glass of wine. 'Yes, of course. Stop fussing. Cheers!' She took a long swig of wine. 'Ah, that's better.'

'Do you think you're turning into an alcoholic, Mum?'

Ruth laughed. 'I don't think so. Not after what Nick's told me. Anyway, if I do I can go to AA with Nick and Amanda. Apparently they have incredible cakes.'

'Yeah, well take it easy with the booze, eh?'

Something came on to the news that caught Ruth's eye. She turned up the volume.

On the screen behind the news anchor was a photograph of Lord Weaver.

'The Conservative peer Lord David Weaver has been arrested at his Kensington home tonight by officers from Scotland Yard. A police spokesman said that Lord Weaver, who is well known for his appearances on television and at celebrity events, is helping officers with their enquiries.'

'That was quick!' Ruth exclaimed.

'Did you know about that?'

'I can't tell you.'

'Oh, top secret is it?' Ella asked, as she screwed up her face and crossed her arms.

Ruth knew that Sergei Saratov and Patrice Le Bon were still at large. They had very dangerous friends and she didn't want to put Ella in any kind of danger.

A sound caught Ella's attention. 'What was that?'

'What was what?' Ruth asked.

Ella went to the curtains that covered the patio doors and looked out. 'I thought I heard a noise.'

'What kind of noise?'

'Like someone was out there.'

Ruth got up from the sofa, and gazed out into the darkness of her garden. She couldn't see anything unusual but she was a little spooked.

'Must be hearing things,' Ella muttered dismissively. She gestured to the hall. 'I'm just going to get my things together before I go.'

'Okay, darling.' Ruth was feeling very unsettled. Sarah might be in witness protection, but the men covering up Gabriela Cardoso's murder had also threatened to kill Ruth. Was she really in danger or was she just being paranoid?

Ella reached for her coat and then looked out of the hall window.

'Are you expecting someone?' she called.

'No, no one. Why?'

'A car just pulled up outside,' Ella said as she reached out to open the front door.

'Don't answer the door Ella!'

'What?'

'Seriously,' Ruth called out as she moved quickly towards the hall. 'Don't answer the door!'

It was too late.

Ella opened the door and turned back to look at Ruth.

Oh God, what's going on?

'Mum!'

'What is it?' Ruth asked as she raced to the door.

'You need to come here,' she said urgently.

Ruth felt the clamp of panic as she reached the door and saw a figure standing in the darkness.

'Sorry. I'm really sorry.'

It was Sarah.

Ruth gave a huge sigh of relief. 'Oh my God. Sarah!'

Sarah winced. 'Is it okay that I'm here?'

Ruth smiled at the absurdity of the question. 'Of course, of course,' she said as she felt the tears forming in her eyes.

Sarah looked at Ella. 'Wow, look at you. You're so beautiful. Come here.'

Sarah and Ella held each other for a few seconds.

'You're meant to be in witness protection!' Ruth said through her tears.

Sarah shrugged. 'I think I might have given them the slip.'

'How did you get here?'

Sarah gestured to the car. 'I got a taxi.'

'From London?'

Sarah grinned. 'Yes. My lovely taxi driver Leon has brought me all the way from Russell Square. It's £275. And I don't have any money, but Leon says he can take a card payment.'

Ruth laughed. 'Oh, he did, did he?'

'I'm so sorry. I just needed to see you,' Sarah whispered as her voice broke and she began to weep.

Ruth held her. 'Money doesn't matter. I'm just really glad you're here.'

Enjoy this book?
Get the next book in the series
'The Lake Vyrnwy' #Book 11
on pre-order on Amazon
https://www.amazon.co.uk/dp/B09H53CYT5
https://www.amazon.com/dp/B09H53CYT5

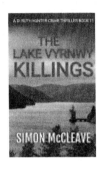

The Lake Vyrnwy Killings
A Ruth Hunter Crime Thriller #Book 11

Your FREE book is waiting for you now

Get your FREE copy of the prequel to
the DI Ruth Hunter Series NOW
http://www.simonmccleave.com/vip-email-club
and join my VIP Email Club

NEW RUTH HUNTER SERIES

London, 1997. A series of baffling murders. A web of political corruption. DC Ruth Hunter thinks she has the brutal killer in her sights, but there's one problem. He's a Serbian War criminal who died five years earlier and lies buried in Bosnia.

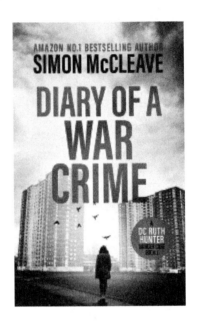

https://www.amazon.co.uk/dp/
B08T654J73
https://www.amazon.com/dp/
B08T654J73

AUTHOR'S NOTE

Although this book is very much a work of fiction, it is located in Snowdonia, a spectacular area of North Wales. It is steeped in history and folklore that spans over two thousand years. It is worth mentioning that Llancastell is a fictional town on the eastern edges of Snowdonia. I have made liberal use of artistic licence, names and places have been changed to enhance the pace and substance of the story.

Acknowledgements

I will always be indebted to the people who have made this novel possible.

My mum, Pam, and my stronger half, Nicola, whose initial reaction, ideas and notes on my work I trust implicitly. And Dad, for his overwhelming enthusiasm.

Thanks also to Barry Asmus, former South London CID detective, for checking my work and explaining the complicated world of police procedure and investigation. Carole Kendal for her acerbic humour, copy editing and meticulous proofreading. My designer Stuart Bache for yet another incredible cover design. My superb agent, Millie Hoskins at United Agents, and Dave Gaughran and Nick Erick for invaluable support and advice.

1 There was a 'seemed to be' repeated below, and in this case 'was' is more appropriate.

2 'get her balance' was repeated above.

3 'soft drinks' was repeated.

4 He's already kicked him in the head so this needs to be a bit different.

Printed in Great Britain
by Amazon

67392896R10132